INHERITING MURDER
A Bobwhite Mountain Cozy Mystery
Mystery
Book 1

JAMIE RUTLAND GILLESPIE

2022 Inheriting Murder by Jamie Rutland Gillespie

For my precious late best friend, Stacey Dennison.
I love you and miss you, Ethel. Save me a seat beside you
on the bench. I will be there when my earthly duties are
done. Until then, I carry you in my heart everyday.

Love,
Lucy

Chapter 1

Landry Burke sat at the desk and tried to smooth her long red hair down. She had grabbed a shower at the hotel and then learned that there was no blow dryer. She had packed so fast when she left her little hometown of Bent Branch, South Carolina that she didn't remember to bring her own dryer. Serious mistake…her hair had a mind of its own.

She looked at her watch. Her Aunt's attorney, Mr. Wilcox, had requested that she report to his office at 9:00am to discuss her Aunt Matilda Jean Mayweather's Will. Landry had only known her as Aunt Tildie and everyone called her that. It seemed that Landry had inherited the entire estate from her Aunt. Landry knew that her Aunt had always thought of her like a daughter and had even paid for Landry's college expenses that were not covered by the scholarships she had earned. But, she was still in shock, not only that she was her Aunt's beneficiary, but that her Aunt had passed away. Yes, Landry knew about the cancer. When she had spoken to Aunt Tildie just 6 months ago, the cancer had been in remission and she said she was doing great. What had happened in such a short amount of time?

As she was thinking about that, she glanced out of the office window and saw Bobwhite Mountain in the distance. She thought about what Aunt Tildie had told her about the history of the mountain and the town. The mockingbird was actually the state bird of Tennessee but when the mountain was named, bobwhite quail were very prevalent in the trees on the mountain. The town below was given the same name as the mountain, and the bobwhite quail was later named the official game bird of the state.

At that moment, the door opened and Mr. Wilcox walked in. He was much younger than he sounded on the phone. He had blonde hair that was a little longer than she would have expected for an attorney. He had piercing blue eyes and was a very handsome man. Landry automatically checked for a ring. Nope. Guess he was too busy being a hotshot attorney to think about marriage at this stage of his life.

"Miss Burke, I"

"Please, call me Landry." She sat up a little straighter and touched her hair again.

"Alright, and I am Adam." He held his hand out to her.

She shook it, smiled and said, "Pleased to meet you, Adam."

"Landry…I have to admit that this is a very unusual estate meeting. What I mean is, the estate requirements are unusual. You see, your Aunt, Matilda Jean Mayweather, has left you the entirety of her estate…but, there are conditions."

"So you said on the phone. Could you just explain everything and then I will ask questions? I am getting a little nervous about all of this."

"Of course. Your Aunt left you an apartment building and…"

"What? An apartment building? I knew she owned the

little bookstore on Main Street. I just assumed that she left that to me since she and I shared a love of books. She was a Librarian at our local library in Bent Branch before she moved to Bobwhite Mountain years ago and she is why I went to school to be a Librarian."

There was a panic attack trying to surface. She had been diagnosed with anxiety when she was just a young child. She asked for a glass of water so that she could take her medication that she had forgotten to take earlier that morning. Adam went to the counter and poured her some water and gave it to her. She reached in her purse and got her medication and took it. "Sorry, I forgot to take my medicine earlier. Please continue."

"Uh, yes. I told you this was an unusual circumstance. She did leave you the bookstore, of course. But, she also left everything else in her estate to you as well, including the apartment building, her personal belongings and what money she had, which is quite substantial. What is unusual about this is that she has required that you take over the apartment building and bookstore within a month of being notified of her intentions. She does not want there to be a long time in between her death and you taking over everything. Smooth transition, she called it. Also unusual is the fact that she has put in the Will that you must show a profit from both establishments at the end of the first year; otherwise, the properties are to be sold and the money donated to her charities of choice."

"So, let me get this straight. My Aunt loved me enough to leave me her entire estate but didn't trust me enough to think I would be successful without the threat of losing it all after putting in my time and effort after a year?"

"Yep. I think that about sums it up. I told you it was unusual." Adam looked down at the floor for a second then looked back up into Landry's brilliant green eyes. "You know, Landry. This may seem like a quiet, little country town, and it is, but we actually have a few people living here or vacation here that are very wealthy. We tend to get the ones who have lots of money but want to walk around unnoticed and not get any special treatment. The ones who are loaded but don't want to act or be treated that way. I mean, we do have the "regular Joes" like you and me and even a few that just can't seem to get on their feet. We are fortunate in that almost every person in this town, whether they live here full time or they vacation here, are relatively kind, caring people. We look after our own in this little mountain town. We make it a point to shop locally most of the time, support our schools and athletic programs and we are very blessed to have the financial support of our part time or full time wealthy residents as well. They know that they will not be made a spectacle of while they are here and that we respect their privacy. They love the small town feel and are comfortable here. In turn, they contribute to the community and treat everyone here the same."

He brushed his hand through his hair like he was trying to think of the right thing to say to convey what he wanted her to know. He continued, "A few have built huge houses up on the mountain and make trips into town every so often. So you see, we have a good variety of people here and we are quite a unique place and strive to keep it that way. I honestly don't think you will have a problem staying solvent in either of the properties you are inheriting. Miss Tildie never had a problem with it at all. Why don't we meet, say around 1pm this afternoon at the bookstore? You can look around there and speak to the 2 part time high school kids that your Aunt had working there for her. Then we will go across the street to the apartment building. Does that sound good to you?"

"Yes. That will be fine." Landry said and suppressed a yawn. "Sorry, I drove straight here through the night from South Carolina. I need to find a place to stay and freshen up. Is there somewhere you can recommend?"

Adam smiled a half smile that for some reason made Landry want to smile back at him. What was wrong with her? She just met this man and he was all business with her, for goodness sakes. It must be the lack of sleep, she thought. She realized that Adam had been speaking and was waiting for an answer from her.

"I'm sorry, what? I guess all of this is just hitting me and I am a little overwhelmed. I am afraid I didn't hear what you were saying." Landry could feel her face redden.

"Totally understandable. What I was saying is that you have an apartment in the building that was your Aunt's. It is now yours, so you will have a place to stay after we get there this afternoon. If you would just like to freshen up and change clothes, maybe lie down for a little bit, my mother actually owns a B&B in town. I will give her a call and tell her to be looking for you. She has an extra room that she always keeps open for my sister, who is a travel nurse. She pops into town on a whim, so my Mom keeps the room open for her. I happen to know that my sister left yesterday for a short assignment in San Diego, so the room is open. When you leave this building, you will turn right and drive about 4 blocks. The B&B has a sign out front. Judith's B&B. Can't miss it. She does great business during spring, summer and fall. And people book years in advance to stay there during our Mountain Christmas Festival. I think it will be what you need for a few hours." Adam stood up and started for the door to open it for her.

"Thank you. That is very kind. I already checked out of my hotel this morning. I had stopped a few towns over early this morning when I realized I needed to freshen up and at least splash some water on my face. I think I was only there for two hours. I was going to find a hotel here to stay after our meeting until I found something permanent. I am sure I will like it here. I sure hope so since I already quit my librarian job in Bent Branch. Of course, I thought I would just be running my Aunt's bookstore. Everything else is a shock but I am open to seeing where it may lead. Thanks again." Landry stood and shook Adam's hand. Then, she turned and went downstairs to get in her teal blue Bug. That is something else she and Aunt Tildie had in common - they both loved Volkswagens.

Chapter 2

Landy realized as she was driving to the B&B that she was very tired. Her eyes were crossing and she could not stop yawning. Just then, she saw a very pretty sign out in front of a large home. This must be it even though she didn't feel like she had driven the 4 blocks that Adam said it was from his building. She hoped she hadn't been 'sleep driving'. She parked her Bug in front and went to the door of the house. She knocked several times and nobody came to the door. Then, it hit her. "Landry, this is a business establishment, like a motel. I should probably just walk in." she said to herself.

She did just that and was surprised. This was a gorgeous home. No wonder Judith was always booked up. She walked around a little and called out, "Judith? Mrs. Wilcox? Is anyone here?" When she got no answer, she decided that Judith must have gone to the grocery store or on some other errand. She sat down on the couch in the living room and decided to wait until Adam's Mom got back.

She must have been so tired that she dozed off. When she opened her eyes, there were several strange people staring at her. "Oh. I'm sorry…I guess I nodded off. Which one of you is Judith?" A lady stepped forward and said, "There is no one by that name here. Can I help you?"

Landry thought for a second and said, "Oh, you must be the other visitors staying here. I was told to meet Judith here at the B&B. Her son spoke with her earlier and she said that I could come and rest awhile and freshen up before my next meeting with him."

The same lady said, "Miss, this is not the B&B. I am Mrs. Jefferies and I am the historian for the town. This is an historical building and I am currently giving a tour. Judith's B&B is a couple of blocks down the road."

Landry was mortified. "Oh no. I am so very sorry." She jumped up and fell flat on the floor. She heard one of the other ladies in the group say under her breath, "It is so disturbing when young people feel the need to imbibe so early in the day."

"What?" Landry got back up. "No. I don't even drink. Well, maybe a glass of wine every once in a while, but not today. I am not drunk. My foot went to sleep and I didn't realize it. Let me gather my things and leave."

She walked out to her car and drove the two blocks to the correct house. Judith greeted her warmly and when Landry told her what had happened, Adam's Mom just laughed and said, "That's probably the only interesting thing those folks will see today. Now, let me show you your room and after you rest up, you can have some lunch before you go."

As Landry left the B&B, she thought about how Adam's Mom, Judith Wilcox, was such a nice person. She made Landry feel right at home and very comfortable. She was glad to have Mrs. Wilcox as a new friend. She hadn't been back to Bobwhite Mountain, Tennessee since she had entered middle school. Landry used to visit her Aunt Tildie during the summers when Landry's Mom, Claire Mayweather Burke, had travel plans. Landry didn't like traveling with Claire since her Mom didn't understand that a child/teenager liked different things to do and places to see than adults. Claire considered herself a Socialite since she divorced Landry's father years before. She was always on the go and had the money to do it since she had inherited a good sum of money from HER Aunt...so did Tildie. Landry had always thought it sad that Aunt Tildie had never married and had children. Claire had told Landry that Aunt Tildie had been very much in love with a young man when she was in her 20's and they had made all sorts of plans to marry. He went to California to interview for a postal position there and had been killed in a car accident. Claire said that Tildie never got over it and never dated anyone again.

The sisters were as different as night and day. Aunt Tildie loved having Landry visit since she had no children of her own. Landry liked visiting since, at that time, her Aunt lived on a working farm. It was so much fun to spend time with the horses, cattle and watch as the helpers would plant or harvest crops. She was very surprised when she heard that Aunt Tildie had bought the bookstore in town. She was even more surprised to learn that later, she had sold the farm and bought an apartment building.

She parked her car in front of the bookstore and got out. She looked up at the name of the place and smiled. "Jasmine Bloom Books'. Aunt Tildie had lived in Bent Branch when she was a child and the jasmine was the state flower of South Carolina. Landry noticed the name of the bookstore was a nod to Aunt Tildie's home state. She loved that.

"Hey, there." Adam was standing just inside the bookstore and waved for her to come in.

She walked to the door to enter and said, "Hey, yourself. Thank you so much for contacting your mother for me. She is a jewel. You really lucked out in the Mom department."

"Yeah, she is pretty special. Let me warn you that she does have a temper if anyone messes with her family, but she hasn't shown that side of her personality since I graduated middle school. She had to set straight a couple of bullies that were out to get me" he laughed. "That was before my growth spurt and before I learned to speak up for myself. She took care of that situation in a skinny minute." He grinned thinking about it and Landry thought it was the nicest grin she had seen in a long time.

"Well, she was the perfect hospitable, southern woman to me. She reminds me of Aunt Tildie in that way. Your Mom seems to enjoy taking care of people. I guess that's why the B&B is such a good fit for her."

They turned and walked further into the bookstore. It was so charming that Landry almost got choked up. She could feel Aunt Tildie's presence in the decor and the smells. Fresh brewed coffee, which she spotted on a table to the side; apples and cinnamon that she was sure was some kind of potpourri simmering in a crockpot; and then something else. She smelled the scent of books. She and her Aunt always swore that that was their favorite scent in the world. It was like she walked into a place she had been before and was destined to be for always. It felt that comfortable. It also made her a little sad since it reminded her of the library she had left back home.

Suddenly, the door flung open and in walked an older man. He was carrying a large bag and, once Landry noticed his uniform, she deduced that he was the mail carrier.

"Hi, Cecil," one of the young girls at the register yelled, "Just a sec and I will get you the mail we have going out today."

The man grumbled something under his breath and began putting packages and mail on the desktop.

Adam took Landry by the arm and walked her over to the man. "Cecil, this is Landry Burke. She is Miss Tildie's niece and has inherited the bookstore as well as the apartment building across the street."

Landry put a big smile on her face and said, "Well, hello Cecil. It is a pleasure to meet you. I imagine we create lots of work for you between the two properties."

Cecil looked up from what he was doing. "Yes. Too much work for an old man. Can't understand how two businesses can create that much crap to mail off. And, you can tell your help that those books are heavy. Need to put fewer in a box so it won't be so hard on me."

About that time, the young girl came back with a ton of packages and mail. "Here ya go, Cecil. Not too much for you today."

Cecil grumbled again, took the mail and put it in the

mailbag, took the packages in his arms and walked out and back to his mail truck.

Adam looked at her sheepishly, "Well, I told you that we had a few residents of our fine town that never got the memo to be nice." He laughed and said, "That right there is one of 'em. Cecil Banks. Mail carrier, grumpy old man and one of the town's biggest gossips. He does have a good heart deep down…or at least that's what we like to think. His wife is a nice lady and tries to keep him in line."

He smiled and turned to the two girls staring at them in anticipation. He said, "Ladies, this is Landry Burke. She is Miss Tildie's niece and now owns the bookstore. "Landry, this" he pointed at the tall thin girl with blonde hair, "is Jenna Shipman. She is a Senior in high school and has worked for Miss Tildie for what is it now, Jenna? How many years?"

"This is my third year here. My grandmother and Miss Tildie are friends. Or, rather, were friends. I am so sorry about your aunt, Mrs. Burke. We loved her very much and will miss her being here." Jenna stared down at the floor.

"Thank you, Jenna. That is very kind of you. Actually it is MISS Burke and I would prefer it if you call me Miss Landry."

"Ok, Miss Landry. I love your name."

Landry smiled and said, "Thanks…well, I guess I should thank my Mom since that is what she named me. It is after my Dad, Landon." She giggled a little to make Jenna feel more comfortable.

Adam spoke up, "And, this is Maisy Penworth." He

motioned to a short girl with short brown hair. She wore glasses and looked to be younger than Jenna. She walked up and stuck her hand out to Landry. "Howdy, BossLady. Very nice to meet ya. I am a freshman in high school and I just started working here 6 months ago. I enjoy my job and I am very thorough with my work. You can depend on me. I am also sorry about your Aunt passing away. She was very good to me and I really liked the old lady."

Adam cleared his throat and Jenna looked mortified. Landry just smiled at Maisy and said, "Thank you very much. I am sure my Aunt loved spending some time with you when she was able to come to the bookstore. Thank you both for your kind words."

"I think we better get on to the apartment building. I have to show you around and I know you want to get settled into your apartment." Adam looked at the girls and said, "Do you two think you can spare a few hours on Saturday to show Landry the ins and outs of this place? I know you both will be valuable resources for her as she has questions about it."

"I absolutely can," said Jenna, "I have nothing planned for this Saturday."

"No can do this Saturday. I have a softball game and then I have to babysit my kid brother for my folks. They are celebrating their anniversary with a night out on the town. Besides, this is Jenna's Saturday to work. You see, we normally each work every other Saturday. Sorry." Maisy shrugged her shoulders.

"No problem at all, Maisy. I will hang out with Jenna

and then maybe another day you and I can talk. IF you are sure you can be here, Jenna. I know Seniors in High School usually have plans."

Jenna turned to Landry. "Yes, Miss Landry. I am positive that I can do it. Like Maisy said, this is my Saturday to work. No problem."

"Great. I will see you here on Saturday at 10 o'clock. Thanks, Jenna. Now, we must go right now but, I will be dropping back in this week for a few minutes at a time. Here is my card with my cell phone number. Please call me if a problem comes up. See you later, girls." Landry and Adam walked to the door and stepped outside. Landry shielded her eyes and looked across the street at the apartment building. The name over the door said, Magnolia Place Apartments. Landry just smiled. Aunt Tildie was completely in love with the huge Magnolia tree outside of the small library where she worked in Bent Branch. It would bloom and have the prettiest flowers that smelled heavenly. Landry remembered her Aunt saying when she decided to move to Bobwhite Mountain to buy the farm, that the only two things she would miss were Landry and that big ole Magnolia Tree. She loved the fact that her Aunt named the apartment building as a homage to that tree.

They walked across the street and Adam started to open the door to the apartment building. Before he could do it, a very tall man with wavy gray hair and dressed in a suit opened it for them. "Hello, Mr. Wilcox. And, this must be Miss Burke. Adam told us you were coming today. It is a pleasure to meet you. I am Garrett Smith, one of your two doormen for the building."

"It is so good to meet you, Garrett. Please call me Landry."

"Uh, if you don't mind, I would prefer to call you Miss Burke. You see, I am of the old school and like to refer to my employer by their last name. If you approve, of course."

"That is fine, Garrett. I actually applaud your manners and your respect."

Garrett bowed his head a little and walked away. He went back to the counter where he positioned himself to see anyone who might enter the building.

Landry thought to herself that he was all business. Guess that's what was needed for someone who let people into an apartment building. She approved of him immediately. She turned around and somehow her heel got stuck on something and she tumbled to the floor right at Adam's feet. He looked shocked but reached down and picked her up.

"Sorry, I forgot to mention that I am accident prone. I was born clumsy. Even the 3 years of social training that my Mother forced me to do was not enough to change that. Thanks for helping me up." Landry's face was red...she could feel it. Great first impression for the employees.

Adam just smiled at her and turned to the young woman standing by the desk on the right hand side of the entrance. "Landry, this is Lisa Wilcox. She is the Office Manager here."

Landy shook the young woman's hand. Lisa was a very pretty woman. Blonde hair that came just below her shoulders and a smile that lit up the room. She was wearing slacks and a gorgeous short sleeved sweater that was robin's egg blue and shimmered when she moved.

"So pleased to meet you, Lisa. Wilcox? Are you related to Adam?" Landry thought to herself that this must be Adam's wife. So many men didn't wear their wedding rings these days and, honestly, these two looked like they belonged together.

Lisa laughed and said, "Guilty as charged. Adam and I are cousins. Our fathers are brothers."

Adam spoke up, "When my father left my Mom, me and my sister, Ivy, without a word and never looked back, Lisa's father became like a Dad to me. Lisa and I were practically raised together like brother and sister."

"Yep, we also fought like brother and sister, too." Lisa gave Adam a quirky little grin.

"By the way, where is Fred? Is he here today?" Adam turned to Garrett.

"He is supposed to be. He comes in at 1pm to relieve me but we haven't seen or heard from him." Unusual, really. He is almost never late. Did you try calling him yet?" Garrett looked at Lisa expectantly.

"I did. I only have his cell phone number since he doesn't have a landline anymore. It just rings and rings with no answer. I even tried calling his sister, Melodie. No answer there but that is not unusual since she goes out of town for work on a regular basis."

Landry looked concerned and curious at the same time. "Oh, I am sorry, Landry. You must wonder who we are talking about." Adam said. "Fred Leiton is the other doorman for the building."

"Fred normally works from 1pm until 11pm. Garrett comes in at 4am and works until 1pm. Garrett refuses to take a lunch hour, so he stays an hour less than Fred. We had a part timer that came in at 11pm and stayed until 4 but he quit on us and Miss Tildie decided to not replace him. We don't have many folks coming and going during that time." Lisa explained to Landry. "Fred and Garrett both do other things besides just being doormen. They are the only employees now, besides me, two maintenance men, and part time housekeepers that come in a few times a week."

"Anyway, I am the Manager which means I do the payroll, rent the apartments, collect the rent, keep the ledgers, handle marketing and lots of other things to keep the place running smoothly. If you can spare a day soon, you should come to see me and I can explain everything that I do here. Miss Tildie was my backup if I ever had to take time off. She knew what everybody did better than we did." Lisa gave a sad smile. "I am sure going to miss seeing her."

"Well, I guess I need to show you the rest of the building and also where your apartment is. I know you have to be tired." Adam looked at Landry.

She shrugged, "I am SO tired, but I want to see just what I now own. This is all still so overwhelming."

She looked at her watch. It was now almost 3pm. She had been up a very long time, except for the few hours she slept at Judith's B&B. She was running on adrenaline at this point and was very glad that she had taken Judith up on a lunch of soup and a sandwich.

Chapter 3

Adam and Landry entered the elevator and he began to tell her things about the building. "Your Aunt took me on a tour one day to show me the building. She wanted me to be able to explain as much to you as I could in the event that she passed away. Lisa took the liberty of providing me with a map of the building and some info about it. I am truly thankful that she did since, I will admit, I probably didn't pay as much attention to detail as I should have when Miss Tildie was showing me around." Adam looked like a little boy who had been scolded.

Landry just laughed at that and waited for him to begin her enlightenment of the building she had inherited.

"So, it is actually much smaller than you probably imagine it to be. There are five floors. The first floor is the office/lobby area, as you saw. Also, there is a parking deck on the right hand side as you go out of the elevator. Two parking spaces for each apartment. There is also a small storage building for each apartment that is located behind the parking spaces. Miss Tildie bought some of those grocery carts that stores use. She put one for each apartment in the cart corral that is in the corner of the parking deck. Makes it easier for the residents to unload their groceries and things into the cart and take it up to their apartment. I thought that was an ingenious idea." He smiled but didn't look up from his notes.

"Residents?" Landry asked. "Do you mean the tenants

that rent the apartments?"

"Yes, but your Aunt preferred to call them residents. She said this was their home and that they chose to reside here when they could live anywhere else. She loathed the word 'tenant'. She was a people person and she always treated all of the residents and employees with the utmost respect."

"I love that." said Landry and Adam continued on.

"On the left hand side as you walk out of the elevator, there is a door that leads to a small patio with a water fountain, a couple of tables and a few built-in grills. It is against code for anyone to grill on their balcony but, Miss Tildie worked with the Fire Inspector to put that area far enough away so that if any of the residents wanted to grill out, they could do it there." They had long ago reached the second floor. He was holding the door open while he finished that part of the orientation process.

He then continued. "The second and third floors have six apartments each. They are all two bedroom apartments. The fourth floor has only three apartments. Two of those are one bedroom and the third is the owner's apartment. That will be yours now. It has two bedrooms and is slightly larger than any of the others. It includes an office and a den. The two one bedroom apartments on that floor are both rented by people who live out of town. They pay for the apartment just as if they lived here full time, though. One resident is an Author who comes here whenever she needs to have peace and quiet to write. Usually, nobody except Lisa even knows she is in town. The Author orders her food and supplies and has them delivered to the lobby and one of the doormen brings them to the 4th floor and leaves a cart outside her apartment. Lisa rings her up and lets her know. When she is done emptying the cart, she rings Lisa back and puts the cart back outside the door for Fred or Garrett to pick it up. When she leaves, she lets Lisa know to call a local maid to come and clean the apartment for the next time she shows up."

"Wow." Landry replied. "How long has she rented the apartment and had this routine?"

"According to Lisa, for several years now."

"What about the other apartment on that floor?"

"Well," Adam said, "that one is even more secretive than the first. Seems a gentleman who works for a security firm and sets up arrangements for his company to install security for businesses and homes in this part of the state rents that one. He is in and out when he is in the area. He actually lived here as a boy for a while and loves the town. Before we go up to the 4th floor for me to show you your apartment, let's go to the 5th floor. No apartments are there, but I think you will be interested to see what is there."

Landry couldn't imagine what she was about to see next.

They got back in the elevator and hit the button. When they stepped out, there was a door in front of them. Adam used a key card that Lisa had given them and opened it. Landry's eyes got huge.

"Adam. This is gorgeous."

Adam grinned and said, "I thought you would like it. When Miss Tildie bought the building, this was just a storage area. She decided to remodel it and make it an 'Event Room'. Businesses in town rent it out for special events like Christmas parties, retirement parties, awards celebrations, even wedding showers or receptions."

Landry barely heard him as she took in the beautiful room. It was decorated in white and silver. The couches and chairs were a mixture of light mauve and cream colors. They were exquisite. Half of the room was carpeted and the other half had gleaming wood floors and the coordinating drapes were breathtaking. There was a podium set up and a large screen as well as a projector. The silver tables and white accents in the room were perfect. Landy had never seen such a wonderfully decorated area. And, it was huge. The seating area on the wood floor side of the room could be moved to make a dancing area that would fit a large party.

"Lisa handles the renting of the room and coordinates with the renters to make sure that everything is just as they want it. Did you notice the artwork on the walls?" Adam asked.

At that moment, Landry took in all the paintings that filled the room. Magnolia paintings. Magnolia blooms, magnolia trees, landscapes with magnolia trees in the background. They were all framed in the most extravagant silver frames she had ever seen. She got teary eyed and looked at Adam.

"Your Aunt collected many of these over the years.

She also spoke with our local art gallery owner Sylvia Weathers, who buys and sells paintings, many of which are locally painted and some that are very famous worldwide. She told her what she was looking for and Sylvia found some of the more expensive ones here. She also then arranged framing for her with the special silver frames. Miss Tildie paid greatly for them, but she told me that this was always her dream. She said she would daydream about owning a room like this decorated in just this way. When she finally got the money, she did it. She told me that she charged very well for the use of the space and that many visitors from out of town even reserved the space for special occasions. I have to say, it IS very lavish. Our law firm has had our Christmas party here for the last few years."

"It is just amazing. I am so glad that Aunt Tildie got to see her dream come to fruition. I feel humbled and honored that she left this to me. I know it had to be her pride and joy. What is behind that door?" Landry pointed at a door on the far end of the room.

"Oh yeah. That is the kitchen area for the event room. It is very well appointed and can handle all kinds of preparation and cooking for large as well as small events. Here, let me show you."

Adam pushed open the door and stopped so fast in his tracks that Landry, who was still looking behind at the alluring Event Room, ran right into his back. "Oh, sorry," she said, "I wasn't expecting you to stop so fa...."

The next thing that was heard was a loud, guttural

scream. It took a minute for Landry to realize that it was coming from her. There in the middle of the floor of this gleaming, perfectly decorated kitchen was a man. He was laying in a puddle of blood and a knife was still sticking out of his chest.

Chapter 4

The panic attack was brutal. Landry could not get a breath in. She was shaking all over. She felt like she would pass out at any moment. Adam pushed her into the nearest chair in the Event Room and bent down in front of her.

He spoke low, slow and even. "Landry, I need you to focus on your breathing exercises. Don't those help with panic attacks? Think about something calming and breathe in and out slowly. Can you do that for me? I have some things I have to do pretty quickly here and I need you here with me."

Landry reached down and touched the rings on her finger. She started spinning the middle one. This was one of her coping mechanisms when she had a panic attack. It always helped. She spun that ring around and around and breathed through her nose and out through her mouth. She noticed a few water bottles on the table across the room.

"Water," she said to Adam and pointed toward the table. He immediately got up and grabbed one for her. She gulped down some water and when he squatted back down to look at her, she focused on those bright, blue eyes of his. She wasn't actually even looking IN them, she was using them as her focal point. She breathed in and out a few more times. "I think I am ok for now. What do we need to do?"

Adam blew out a big breath that it seemed like he had been holding since this started. "I need to call Lisa and tell her what we just found. I have to get her to call the

Sheriff's Department and get them here ASAP. I also want her to lock the elevator to this floor so that nobody can access this area except for the authorities. I have no idea if there is an event scheduled for tonight, but I don't want anybody coming up here. Just sit here for now and try to keep calm."

He picked up his cell and phoned Lisa. He explained what he and Landry had found and told her to call the Sheriff's Department and lock the elevator. He listened to her for a minute and said, "Uh, yeah, I do. It's Fred."

Landry looked up at him. "Oh my gah.. It is one of my employees?" She jumped up and that is when the dizziness hit. She fell flat on her face on that pretty wood floor. Adam came running and picked her up. She had a bloody nose and it felt to her like a tooth was loose. When she fell, she also twisted her ankle and it was throbbing. She grabbed the ankle and with gritted teeth yelled, "I am so clumsy."

Adam was taken aback. "Landry, you got dizzy. Calm down."

"Calm down…calm down? I am sleep deprived, my nose is bleeding, I think I broke a tooth and I just found out that an employee of an apartment building that I found out today I now own, has been murdered in the kitchen. How am I supposed to calm down?" She was hysterical at this point.

Adam stared at her and thought better of telling her that she also had a huge gash on her head and one of her eyes was surely going to be black very soon.

Instead, he did the only thing he could think of. He got out his handkerchief and wiped blood off her nose. Then, he went to the counter where he got the water bottle and grabbed some napkins and told her to put them on the front of her head and keep pressure on it.

Right about then, the door burst open and three men in uniforms ran in. They stopped in their tracks when they saw Adam and Landry. "Oh, we thought Lisa said there was a body. I see you revived her."

Landry groaned and Adam rolled his eyes. "She is not the victim, Wyatt. I will explain this later. The body is in the kitchen through that door. It's Fred Leiton."

The three men went into the kitchen. Adam said, "You probably won't remember all these names but the guy who I was talking to is the Sheriff. His name is Wyatt Collins. Gruff around the edges but excellent at his job. The other two are deputies. The one with the mustache is Ben Coleman and the other one is Tyler Grimes. They are as good as they come. I know they will get to the bottom of all of this. Landry, I really hate that this happened on your first day here. Believe me when I say that this is not the kind of thing that happens here a lot. I mean, I can't remember the last murder we had."

Landry grunted and said, "Well, there is something you should know about me Adam. I am kind of a jinx. I mean, things just seem to...happen...whenever I am around. My first week at the Library in Bent Branch, the roof started leaking and part of the ceiling came down right in the lobby; then, when they were repairing that, somehow one of the roofers slipped and fell onto the concrete in front of the huge plate glass window which just happened to be located in the Children's area during reading hour. The poor roofer was ok after he got a cast all the way up to his sternum. They got the roof repaired and all was going great until two months later when the tornado came through and took off said roof and ruined hundreds of books. That is just one example of bad things happening when I am around. It's been that way my whole life. I guess that's why I have anxiety so bad. Waiting for the next shoe to fall and all that."

Adam looked at her. "C'mon, Landry. Those are just coincidences. You are not a jinx. He smiled.

Landry could just imagine what she looked like right now knowing everything that had happened to her and also knowing her "hair that had a mind of its own" had to be disgusting by now. But, she smiled at him anyway and said thank you. "I bet you will be so glad to get rid of me after just this one day."

Adam didn't have time to answer since Wyatt yelled for him from the kitchen. "Coming." He got up and went to the kitchen.

"Adam, did you or the lady see anybody else when you got off the elevator on this floor?" Wyatt asked.

"First of all, the lady has a name. She is Landry Burke. Miss Tildie's niece. Landry inherited this apartment building, as well as Jasmine Bloom Books, from Miss Tildie's estate. I was Miss Tildie's attorney and was showing Landry around a bit today since she had no idea her Aunt even owned an apartment building. To answer your question, no. We didn't see anybody at all."

Two more men and a woman entered the kitchen. Wyatt briefed them and told them to brush for prints and collect any evidence they found after the body had been inspected and moved to the morgue. About that time, the Coroner arrived.

"Hey, Margie" Wyatt greeted her. "We haven't touched anything yet. These guys just arrived. As soon as you inspect the body and get him out of here, they will begin collecting evidence. Victim is Fred Leiton...the doorman here."

"Got it. I won't be too long." Margie took control of the scene.

"Listen, Wyatt" Adam said, "Landry has had an awful long day. I still haven't even shown Landry where her apartment is. You think we could come down to the station in the morning to give our statements?"

"That will be fine, Adam. Just be there after 10. I have a meeting at 8am and I know the mayor will want to be updated on this situation. Wyatt rolled his eyes, sighed and said, "You know how long winded he is."

"Thanks, Wyatt. See you then."

Adam walked back into the Event Room. "Uh, Landry? Wyatt said we could give our statements in the morning at the station. How about I show you to your apartment now? You can rest there."

Landry stood up and her knees were shaking as she tried to walk. She was still a little wobbly, but she forced herself to stay upright. She just wanted a bath and to lie down. She was bone tired.

When they got to her apartment, Adam said, "Lisa had a maid come in and freshen everything up a few days ago. Miss Tildie's things are still in here. We figured you would want to go through them and see what you wanted to keep." Adam looked at her with a sad look on his face. "By the way, your Aunt died in the hospital. Didn't know if anyone had told you that. Lisa still ordered a new mattress and bed covers for your bed. I hope that is alright."

Landry smiled at him, "That is fine, Adam. I don't think I have told you but I do appreciate everything you have done for me today. I have no idea how I would have managed without your help."

"No need to thank me. I actually enjoyed it. Well, until that last part anyway. I really loved Miss Tildie, Landry. She and I had a standing appointment at the K&L diner in town for lunch on Fridays before the cancer treatments made her so weak. She was a pickle, you know, and I enjoyed hearing all of her stories. The more I hang around you, the more you remind me of her." He smiled and turned away. "Anyway, on my way out of the building, I will tell Lisa to order you a plate from the diner and have them bring it to you. She and Garrett refused to leave until the authorities have left the building. Eat the food, take a hot bath and then go to sleep. I will be by to pick you up around 9:30 in the morning so that we can go to the Sheriff's Department. Oh, and if you will give me your keys to your car, I will get Garrett to run across the street and bring it to the parking deck for you. He can bring your keys back when your food comes."

As Landry went to her purse for the car keys, Adam added, "Landry I really am sorry that today was so terrible. I hope you grow to love this little town. I know they will love and welcome you."

"Thanks, Adam. Thanks for everything. Tomorrow is a new day and I am looking forward to it being a better one." She smiled and Adam walked out the door.

Landry turned to take in the apartment. It was roomy but cozy at the same time. Her Aunt had excellent taste and the apartment reflected that. She roamed from room to room taking it all in. When she was done, she phoned Lisa and asked her to please wait about thirty minutes to order the food. She had to get a shower and wash the dried blood from her face. She went into the bathroom and looked in the mirror. She looked like the frightening child clown from the scary movie she watched as a kid. Her red hair was standing straight up on top of her head. Dried blood from her nose and the gash on her forehead was caked up all over. Her eyes were bloodshot and had dark circles under them. "How in the world did the people who had seen her not stare at her in horror?" she thought. She got in the shower and turned the water as hot as she could stand it.

Once she was done, she put on a pair of sweatpants that she found in Aunt Tildie's things. She also found a T-shirt that had magnolias on it and smiled as she put it on. She grabbed a pair of socks and then pulled her still wet hair back in a bun. She was thrilled to see that Aunt Tildie had a blow dryer in the bathroom. That would sure be nice in the morning. She looked to see what she might be able to wear tomorrow so that she wouldn't have to retrieve her suitcases from the car before she went to the Sheriff's Office. She found a pair of jeans that were only a little bit too big for her and a sweater set that was a pale yellow and very soft. She knew that her Aunt only bought the best, while Landry herself loved to shop at thrift stores and discount stores. Luckily, she and her Aunt wore the same size shoe and she found a new pair of keds in the closet that still had the tag on them. Those would work great since her ankle was throbbing and would probably still be in the morning. She heard the ringing of her cellphone in the apartment. She walked carefully on her hurt ankle and picked up the phone as she grimaced. Lisa said, "Landry, the food is here. I took the liberty of ordering you a sweet tea and some coffee. You can reheat the coffee in the morning. Garrett has already put your car in the parking deck and he wants to know if you need him to bring the things you have packed in there up to you now?"

"That is so kind of you both, Lisa. Tell Garrett that we will wait until tomorrow to unload my things. I am fine for tomorrow…I found a few things of Aunt Tildie's to tide me over."

"Great." Lisa continued, "We emptied out the fridge the day they brought the new mattress and then I ordered a few staples to put back in it after the maid cleaned it. So, you should find some things in there until you get to the store to stock up. Garrett will be up in a minute to bring your food and your car keys. Try to get some rest, Landry. I know you have to be so tired."

"Tell you what, Lisa. I will do just that if you promise me that you and Garrett will leave for home as soon as he comes back down. Thank you so much for everything today. I know why my Aunt chose you to manage this building. You handle everything with such ease and grace."

"Thanks, Landry. That means a lot to me. I promise we will leave when Garrett gets back down here. See you tomorrow." Lisa hung up.

The knock at the door startled Landry even though she was expecting it. She opened it and Garrett handed over her food, drink and keys. He stood up tall and said, "There you are, Miss Burke. I hope you have a restful evening. I am very sorry for everything that has happened on your first day here."

"Garrett, were you close with Fred? What I mean is, do you know if there was someone he mentioned that might have had it out for him?"

"No, Miss Burke. I cannot think of him mentioning anyone, enemy or otherwise. Mr. Leiton was a very quiet person. I have known him for years and I will be honest. He is the last person I would think something like this would happen to. He stuck to himself and was a pleasant man, albeit a man of few words. I am sorry this happened to him. Goodnight now, Miss Burke. You need to get your rest. I will see you tomorrow." Garrett nodded his head and went back to the elevator.

Landry closed the door and went to the kitchen. It was

a nice area with updated appliances and a white, round dining table with mismatched chairs that fit perfectly in the room. She opened her bag from the diner and was pleasantly surprised. One of her favorites…fried chicken, rice with gravy, fried okra, coleslaw and a roll. They had even included a slice of lemon pie. This was one of the meals that Aunt Tildie used to cook for her when she visited the working farm that her Aunt owned when Landry was little. Of course, she only ate this kind of meal occasionally now when the craving hit her. It was perfect for her first full meal in Bobwhite Mountain.

She finished her meal, put the take out plate in the trash and as she washed her hands, she remembered that Adam had said that the apartments had balconies. She walked into the living room and pulled back the drapes. Sure enough, there was a sliding glass door.

She went out on the balcony and froze for a second at the sight. There was the huge mountain in the distance with lights from houses scattered around. It had since turned completely dark outside and the view was breathtaking. It looked like the mountain was covered with fairy lights. "I cannot believe this is my home now." she whispered aloud to herself. "This is amazing."

She sat down in one of the chairs on the balcony as the cool air blew slightly. It even smelled different in the mountains. Cleaner, fresher and if she hadn't just seen a murdered man today with a knife protruding from his heart, this would seem like heaven to her.

It must have been hours later when she woke up

shivering. The air had gotten even cooler. The bath, the food and the peaceful view had put her right to sleep. She got up and went inside. As she locked the glass door, she thought about Fred. How horrible for him to die the way he did. Who in the world could just kill a person and leave them there? Who had it out for Fred? She, of course, knew nothing of the man but since he had met his demise in her apartment building, she knew she wouldn't rest until she figured out who had done this.

She went to her bedroom. The new mattress and new bed clothes included a plush, down comforter. She set her alarm for early in the morning and then sank down and snuggled up in that dreamy comforter and sighed with content. She started rubbing her feet together like she had done since she was a child. She went right to sleep.

Chapter 5

The alarm went off at 6. She had 3½ hours to herself until Adam picked her up to head to the Sheriff's department.

She got up and immediately grabbed the cup of coffee out of the fridge that she had saved from last night's take out meal. She popped it into the microwave and was thrilled to notice a coffee maker on the counter. She opened up some cabinets and found Aunt Tildie's stash of coffee and filters. Landry normally had a coffee in her hand all day long and since yesterday was the exception, she figured that was why she had such a throbbing headache right now. She went ahead and made the coffee pot and turned it on while simultaneously taking the cup out of the microwave and downing it in just a few gulps.

Then, she headed to the bathroom to splash some water on her face. She looked in the mirror and thought, "Yeah…lack of coffee is probably not the only reason my head feels like it was bashed in. It also looks like it was." The gash on her forehead didn't look that bad itself, but the bruising was atrocious and her nose was still a little swollen. Her tooth felt sore but, as she brushed her teeth with the items Lisa had put in a baggie in the bathroom for her to use until she got her personal things brought up, the tooth didn't feel loose. Her ankle was still tender, too.

She took another look at herself and decided that it was what it was. She couldn't do anything about any of it since her makeup case was in the parking garage of her car. She could, however, try to tame the beast that was her hair. She wet it and grabbed her brush from her purse. She turned on the blow dryer and did the best she could to make it look decent. Then, she grabbed a clip from her purse and pulled the red curls up on the back of her head. Not so bad. Not so great, but not so bad. It would have to do.

She walked back to the kitchen and grabbed a coffee cup from the cabinet. She filled it up and went back to the den where she had left her cell phone. She had the number of the place that had come and packed up all of her things into some sort of little metal square building and put it in storage until she called and told them where to deliver it. She checked the clock - 7am. She would wait until at least 8 to call since they probably had not arrived at work yet.

Even though her ankle was tender, she decided to go around the apartment and gather some things that she needed to get rid of and while she was at it, she would move things around to work better for her. Since she and Aunt Tildie had practically the same taste in decor, it didn't take long at all to do that. Then, she had gathered up clothes from the closet and would donate those since she didn't find much that would suit her. Most were too big (like the jeans she would be wearing today). She didn't have too many furniture pieces coming with her things, so most of the furniture would stay in the apartment. She had rented a furnished apartment in Bent Branch with the intention of buying a home in the next few years. All she really had in storage was the rest of her clothes, personal items and a few small side tables that she had found at an estate sale a few months back. She loved those tables and would work them into the apartment.

Her books she owned were the main reason she had to store items and didn't have the room in her tiny car to bring them with her. They had filled 4 bookcases in the rental house. Two of those were hers and were also in storage and the other two came with the house and had to stay there. Most of the books were signed by the authors and they were her prize possessions. Between being a librarian and being single and free to travel to book signing events on the weekends, she had amassed a large collection. She would be glad to get her things back with her.

By the time she had finished gathering and organizing, it was 8:10. She called the storage business and gave them her new address. They told her that they would have her things with her by Thursday. This was Tuesday, so that seemed very reasonable to Landry. She walked out on the balcony to check the weather. It had warmed up since the middle of the night when she had woken up in the chair. It seemed to be in the mid 50's to her. This was April in the mountains so it was a little warmer than she would have expected. The short sleeved sweater set of Aunt Tildie's that she was going to wear should be perfect. She turned and went to dress for the day.

At about 9:10, Landry heard a buzzing coming from the living room. A loud buzzing. She moved as fast as she could with her ankle the way it was from the den to see what in the world it was. She got to the living room and heard it again, but had no idea what to do. Then, she heard

Lisa's voice. Landry whipped around, thinking that Lisa had entered her apartment. Then it hit her...the intercom by the door. How stupid she was. She hit the button, "Yes, Lisa?"

"Adam is on the way up. Just giving you a heads up."

"Thanks. I appreciate it. Oh, and Lisa, when I get back from the Sheriff's office, I need to bring the things in from my car. Is there a service elevator I should use or do I just use one of the two in the lobby?"

"Yes, we have a large service elevator. But, don't do that yourself. I mean, you can supervise if you like, but I will get one of our maintenance guys to help. He helps people move in and out of the apartments and he knows exactly how to do it. You don't need to be doing so much on that ankle until it heals up. When will your other things arrive?"

"That sounds perfect. I really don't have that much in my car; just a few clothes and some personal things. The other stuff is scheduled to arrive on Thursday. I would really appreciate his help then, too. Thanks, Lisa."

"Sure thing," Lisa replied and hung up.

Right then, a knock came at the door. Landry opened it and saw Adam, who was holding a beautiful, bright flower arrangement.

"What in the world? Those are gorgeous." she cooed.

"Just thought you might need something to brighten up your day since yesterday was pretty bad. I had them go ahead and put them in a vase so you can just sit them on a table and we will get going. How is your ankle today? Are you ok to walk? If not we will drive. The Sheriff's Department isn't too far, so I thought we could walk down so that you can get a feel for Main Street. If you think it will be too much, we can drive."

"My ankle is fine…just a little tender. I found some sneakers in Aunt Tildie's closet that were still in the box." She looked down and smiled at the shoes. They fit me perfectly and I would love to walk and take in Main Street along the way."

As they went through the lobby, Landry stopped and spoke with Lisa. "Could you please put up a flier or something and let all the residents know that I will be having a meet and greet tomorrow night at 6pm? I want to introduce myself and meet all of them. Could you also order in some finger foods and snacks for the occasion? I guess we will have it in the Event Room on the fifth floor. Does that sound alright?"

"It sounds fine," Lisa replied. "But, Landry, remember that you are now the owner of this building. Whatever you want to do is what we will all do. Just let me know and I will arrange it for you, whatever it is."

"I guess I have to get used to the fact that this building is now mine. And, the bookstore, too. I need to go there later today and see what is going on there."

She and Adam left the building and got on the sidewalk. Landry snuck a peek at the bookstore across the street and immediately thought of something. "Adam, since Jenna and Maisy are in school during the day, who works at the bookstore?"

"Oh, I forgot to mention that. Miss Tildie hired one of her dearest friends, Ms. Wells. We all call her Ms. Millie. She is around 60 years old and was a school cafeteria worker until she retired after 40 years of service. She was and is loved by everybody in this town. She works during the week until the part time girls get out of school.

I will tell you, though, she does not play. What I mean is, she speaks her mind and you always know where she stands" Adam laughed.

Landry took another look at the bookstore. Ms. Millie was outside sweeping the stoop and singing to the top of her lungs. Landry thought that Ms. Millie reminded her of someone but couldn't figure out who.

Ms. Millie looked up and saw Adam and Landry. "Hey, Adam. You better put some suntan lotion on today. You know how you always burned and looked like a fresh picked strawberry after recess. That white skin you got doesn't tan…it just burns. Who is your lady friend?"

Adam rolled his eyes as he and Landry walked across the street to meet Ms. Millie. "I know, Ms. Millie, I know. This is Landry Burke. She is Miss Tildie's niece and the new owner of the bookstore and the apartment building."

"Well, butter my biscuit." Ms. Millie said, "I guess that means you are my new boss." At that moment, it hit Landry. "Ms. Millie. I thought I recognized you. I haven't seen you since I was around 10 years old. I remember you coming to visit Aunt Tildie on the farm. The two of you were best friends."

Ms. Millie smiled real big. "Yep. You were just a little

thing when I first met you. Always seemed nervous to me but, Tildie said it was because of your parents arguing all the time. That farm seemed like a sanctuary to you, child. Tildie and I were both sad when you stopped visiting."

She looked Landry straight in her eyes, "Now, just so you know. I only work from 9 till 3:30 on weekdays. That's it. I don't fill in for anybody or work a minute over. I have a life away from here, ya know. Anyway, I bring my lunch everyday and take my break at 12 sharp. I eat in the backroom and I lock the door and put a sign up. Been doing it that way for years and I don't plan to change that now." Ms. Millie's dark brown eyes were sharp and Landry could tell she meant business.

"That's perfectly fine with me, Ms. Millie.," Landry smiled.

"Good, but that ain't all. Twice a year, I go visit my daughter and grandkids. Tildie always worked my shift those two weeks. Now, you can do that or you can find somebody that needs to get out of the house for a couple of weeks. I will leave them instructions. I don't go again until September, so there is plenty of time to worry about that. You got any questions for me?"

Landry stammered, "Uh...no. Except, I guess, do you like working here?" She couldn't think at that moment since Ms. Millie had been talking so fast it made her head swim.

"Whew, chile.. I love it. I get to hear all the local gossip and I get to meet some of them biggity people that come in here to 'browse'. You best believe by the time those rich people leave, they got a bag of books that I convinced them they had to have." She was referring to the few wealthy folks that had built some big houses on the top of the mountain.

She gave a belly laugh and hit her thigh with her hand. "Well, I gotta go get back to work now. Adam, you show my new boss around but don't get any ideas about gettin' all lovey dovey with her. You got to let others in town get to know her, too. I know you are a ladies man, but control yourself, boy"

Ms. Millie laughed again and went in the door. Adam turned so red that you would have thought he had been laying out at the beach for days with no sunblock.

"I tried to warn you. She is a card. If she thinks it, it rolls right off her tongue. One thing about it, you always know where you stand with Ms. Millie." Adam laughed.

Landry decided right then and there that she loved Ms. Millie and that she would make her one of her best friends in town. She and Adam continued walking to the Sheriff's department.

When they got there, they were sent directly into Sheriff Collins' office. He was on the phone but quickly told the person he would have to call them back. He gestured for them to sit down and asked if they wanted coffee. Adam said no; Landry said yes.

"So, Miss Burke, how are you liking it here so far? Met any of our fine citizens besides Adam here?"

"A few…mainly employees of mine. I just saw Ms. Millie that works at the bookstore. I actually knew her when I was little and visited Aunt Tildie. Ms. Millie is a character." Landry laughed. "And please call me Landry."

"Yeah, Ms. Millie was telling tales out of school." Adam rolled his eyes.

"Wait, now. She didn't tell that one about me that still haunts me to this day every time I have to walk back in that cafeteria, did she? I would hate to have to lock her up." Wyatt smiled.

"Nope. She was set on embarrassing me this time, Wyatt."

Wyatt choked on his coffee and grabbed a napkin to clean up. He walked to the coffee table and gave Landry her cup of coffee and he put a pastry from the box on his desk on a napkin and offered it to her. She gladly took it since she hadn't had breakfast and was starving.

When he got up to get the coffee, Landry noticed for the first time what big guy Wyatt was. Adam looked to be about six feet and Wyatt had to be at least four inches taller. He seemed like a nice guy and was attractive but she could understand how he could be intimidating as a Sheriff. Wyatt handed her the coffee, she thanked him and he nodded.

He chuckled and asked Adam, "Which one did she tell Landry about?"

"Nothing specific, thank goodness. Just portrayed me as a 'ladies man', which is NOT true, by the way." Adam jerked his head towards Landry.

Wyatt belly laughed and then said, "Well, to be fair, Landry, it was the ladies chasing Adam in school, not the other way around. They were wasting their time, though. Our Adam here was too focused on getting straight A's so that he could become a hotshot lawyer. The only other thing he did was play football." Wyatt said. He didn't even date until after college.

"Wait…the two of you went to high school together?" Landry asked.

"We went to school together from the first grade till graduation from high school." Adam replied. "Wyatt and I have known each other our entire lives."

"Yep. Now, we should get down to business. I need to get a statement typed up from both of you - Cora can do that when we are done here." Wyatt said, referring to one of his deputies, Cora Flint.

Chapter 6

Wyatt flipped open a file and Landry automatically focused her eyes on the contents. She gasped and started breathing heavier. She was spinning that middle ring faster than a speeding car. There was a picture on top of the file of Fred's body. She turned her head away from the file and looked at the floor as Adam noticed her nervousness and decided to jump in.

"Uh, Wyatt. Look, Landry and I saw the vict - uh, Fred, up close and personal yesterday. We really don't need to see the crime scene photos right now." Adam looked at Landry. "Ok if I tell him?" he asked.

Wyatt's eyes got big. "Don't tell me you are an ex-con, Landry. I don't need that kind of complication, especially since you found the vic."

"No. Of course not, Wyatt. What is wrong with you?" Adam looked at Landry again and she responded, "Sure...I just really don't want everyone in town knowing my business before I even meet them in person."

"That's not going to happen, Landry. Wyatt is a good guy, even if he can be stubborn and ornery."

Wyatt gave Adam a "stop it" look and pointed his finger at him.

"Listen, Wyatt, what I need to tell you is that Landry has anxiety. She has coping mechanisms to help her out and she is on medication, but something like seeing a dead body or even that crime scene picture of Fred can trigger it.

Just be aware of that, ok?"

"Absolutely. Thanks for letting me know." Wyatt looked at Landry. "I'm sorry. I honestly didn't realize that the pictures were on the top of the file. Forgive me. Are you alright or do you need to wait until another time for this?"

Landry took a big sip of her coffee. "No, I am fine. It wasn't a full fledged panic attack. It was just a shock to see him again like that. Even though I didn't know him before we found him."

"Understood." Wyatt said. "And, since you just got into town yesterday and didn't know Fred, I don't think there is much you can give me as far as who you would suspect of this. Adam told me that the two of you didn't run into anybody else during the time he was showing you around the building. Is that right?"

"Yes...we didn't see anyone else at all. In fact, I had the thought at the time that I was blessed because the building seemed well kept and quiet. It seemed like everything was in order. We didn't even see anyone coming or going from the apartments at the time."

Wyatt nodded his head. "Miss Tildie ran a tight ship. She didn't put up with foolishness from the residents. In return, she treated all of them with respect and tried to help them in any way she could if they had questions or problems. My own brother and his wife live there on the second floor. Cody and Larissa Collins. My older brother. They tell me that they love it there."

"I didn't know that." Adam said in surprise. "I thought

they still lived in Asheville, North Carolina."

"Nope. Moved back about 6 months ago. Seems Cody got a job with a race team out of Mooresville, NC when he finished up pit school. He works the pits…gasman for the team. Larissa wasn't too happy living so far from her family, so they moved back here. She is going to school to be a teacher and travels to the races when she can. They are hoping to start a family soon, so she wanted to be near her Momma. Anyway, my point is that you inherited a great place, Landry."

"Good to hear, Sheriff." Landry replied.

"I do have some evidence that I am going to tell you both about. For your ears only. Please do not repeat anything I tell you. I don't want things getting out that could interfere with the investigation." Wyatt looked at them both sternly. "Got it?"

They both nodded and Wyatt continued, "Someone used the bathroom on that floor to try to clean up after the murder. There was water everywhere and signs of someone wiping the area up. We are trying to get DNA from the blood we found in the drain pipe there. Hopefully, it won't be too diluted so that we can get a full DNA panel from it. Unfortunately, we have to send it to the state crime lab, so it will be awhile before they get back to us." Landry and Adam both said that they hoped the sample would contain DNA.

"Ok, then," Wyatt said, "I guess there is nothing else you two can give me. As Adam knows, this is a gossiping town. If either of you hears anything that pertains to this case, call me. As soon as you can. This is going to be a hard one to figure out, I am afraid. Thanks for coming in. Cora should be outside the door to get your statements to put on file."

After the statements were done, Deputy Flint led them back to the front door and was sitting down behind the front desk as they left. Landry checked her watch. It was almost noon. She really wanted to touch base with Lisa and then go back to the bookstore and talk with Ms. Millie a little more.

Just then, Adam spoke, "Listen, Landry, I have an appointment with a client at 12:30. I really need to go back to the office to prepare. We have plans to go to lunch afterwards, but I was wondering if you might want to have dinner with me tonight. There is a nice restaurant on the outskirts of town called, The Sky High Tavern. Great atmosphere and the food is delicious. What do you say?"

"I say I better ask Ms. Millie if she thinks I will be safe going out to eat with a known 'ladies man'." Landry laughed. At the look on Adam's face, Landry continued. "I am just kidding. I would love to go to dinner with you tonight. What time should I be ready? Or, I can meet you there if that is easier for you. Interesting name for a restaurant."

"No, no. I will come pick you up around 6, if that works for you. It takes about half an hour to get there."

"Sounds good," Landry replied. "I will see you then. Right now, I am headed back to Magnolia Place to do a few things there."

Adam turned left to walk to his office and Landry turned right to go back to the apartment building. She was making good time when a man ran out of a store and stopped in front of her. She gasped and the man looked stunned for a minute. "Sorry, Miss. I was just going to introduce myself. Ms. Millie told me you were in town. I am the mayor of this fine town. Name's Clinton Cartwright. Nice to meet you Miss…" Landry replied, "Burke. Landry Burke. It is nice to meet you, Mayor Cartwright. This is a very nice town from what I have been able to see in just two short days."

"It is, Miss Burke. And, we want it to stay that way. Seems you have had trouble already at the apartment building since you got here. The Sheriff told me about Fred Leiton. We don't care for murders in our town, Miss Burke."

Landry winced and said, "I am sure you don't Mayor Cartwright. I don't care for them in any capacity. If you are insinuating that it is MY fault that a man happened to be killed in my apartment building the day I arrived in town, then you are wrong. I had never even met Fred and furthermore, I doubt that even if I had been here for a year or longer, I could have prevented what happened. His death has nothing to do with me or my apartment building. Now, if you will excuse me, Mayor, I have business to attend to."

Landry walked off. She began shaking and was having trouble breathing. She had never had to be so rude to somebody but, she meant that the Mayor would not think that he could push her around just because she was new here. Nope. Not gonna happen. She smiled and felt herself calming down. It kind of felt good to stand up for herself.

By the time she made it back to the apartment building, her ankle was throbbing again. She said hello to Lisa and Garrett and went upstairs to take some over the counter pain medicine and hoped that would help. When she got back to the lobby, she entered Lisa's office.

"Lisa, could you put an advertisement in the paper for a new doorman for Fred's position and also for a part time doorman to cover the other hours? I really would like to have someone in the lobby 24/7. I guess you have the records showing what the pay is?"

Lisa smiled. "I do. In fact, I already have the ad typed up to send to the local paper and also to the local radio station that puts help wanted ads on their website and I will change it to include the part time position, too. I didn't want to actually send it in until you were ready, though."

"You are a lifesaver, Lisa. I am so glad my Aunt hired you. Also, do any of the employees ever use the kitchen or bathroom on the fifth floor. I mean, do they eat lunch in the kitchen or anything like that?"

"Absolutely not. Miss Tildie was adamant about that. That floor was reserved for events only. The only time any employees were to go to that floor was when it needed maintenance or cleaning.

"Wow…that sounds ironclad. I can understand Aunt Tildie not wanting that area to get messed up, though. It looks like she spent a lot of effort to remodel and make it a showcase. Did you happen to get the flyers made for the meet and greet tomorrow night?"

"Yep. We have an enclosed bulletin board that we put announcements on. It is right between the elevators…I am sure you probably haven't even noticed, but our residents know to check it every time they are in the lobby. I also taped one to each apartment just to be sure. Landry, if I may suggest it, maybe it would be better if you had the meet and greet in the conference room."

"Wait…we have a conference room?" Landry laughed. "I absolutely think it will be better. Where is the conference room located?" Lisa got up and started walking. "Follow me."

They walked around and behind Lisa's office. There was an innocuous door there and when Lisa opened it, there was a huge conference table with chairs and there were also several other smaller, round tables.

"This was an empty room that the previous owners before Miss Tildie used for their own personal storage space. When she bought them out, she remodeled this room and made it a space for residents to use for birthday parties for their kids or other things that may come up. They still do that if they wish, but we also have building meetings as well as employee meetings here." Lisa informed her.

"I guess Aunt Tildie thought of almost everything. The one thing I do want to do after I speak with the accountant that Adam is introducing me to next week is to see about getting security cameras for the whole building, including the parking garage and Event Room. They sure would have been helpful with this murder."

Lisa agreed and Landry said, "I am going up to my apartment now. I just took some pain meds and I am hoping it helps my ankle."

She looked at the clock on the wall to see that it was 1:30. "I think I will lie down for about an hour and then I want to go see Ms. Millie for about an hour before the girls get to the bookstore today. By the way, Lisa, I love your outfit today. You dress so well."

"Thanks, Landry. I am single, so I kind of splurge on myself. I like to look nice. I hope your ankle feels better when you get back up. Oh, and I hope you don't mind but Garrett and one of the maintenance guys took your things from your car and put them in your living room for you."

"Oh, I don't mind at all. I am very grateful to them. I will get everything organized one day." She laughed and headed to the elevator.

When she entered her apartment, she breathed in the sweet smelling air. It smelled wonderful. She looked over at the flowers that Adam had brought her and smiled. They really were very pretty. She then looked into the living room at all of her things from the car. That will get done later, she thought.

She stopped by the bathroom and then went to her bedroom and took off her jeans and sweater set. She put her t-shirt that she slept in last night back on, took the clip from the back of her hair, set her alarm for 2 and and curled up into the luxurious comforter. It was cool in the apartment...just like she loved and the comforter felt so good.

Chapter 7

When the alarm went off, Landry groaned and stretched. She probably shouldn't have taken that nap. Her ankle was still tender and now her head was throbbing again. She got up and went to the kitchen where she poured a cup of coffee and put it in the microwave. Her stomach grumbled and she realized that all she had eaten that day was that pastry at the Sheriff's office early this morning. This was not like her at all. She loved food. Really loved it.

She went to the fridge and saw a carton of eggs, some milk, shredded cheese, a bottle of kalamata olives and a pack of sandwich ham. She took it all out and checked the dates just to be sure. Just like Lisa had said, they were all just stocked recently. She reached down and found a small frying pan and looked in cabinets until she found a bottle of olive oil. Omelet it would be.

She got her coffee out and drank it while she was cooking. She found a glass and poured some of the milk in it. The omelet was perfect and it, along with the milk, filled her up. She put the dishes in the sink and went to throw back on the clothes she had worn earlier today. It hit her that she hadn't decided what to wear tonight.

She went back to Aunt Tildie's closet and looked at the clothes she had left there that she thought she could wear. She pulled out a plain black dress that was about knee length. No, she thought, that looks too formal. She looked at a few others and then finally noticed the long skirt. It had corals, teal, and cream in it and felt like silk. It was still in the dry cleaning bag from the last time it was cleaned. Next to it, there was a coral colored short sleeved sweater that went perfectly with the long skirt. As she took them both out to hang on the back of the bedroom door, she noticed the pearl necklace. It was strung around the hanger of the sweater. Landry smiled. Aunt Tildie had always done this when she hung up a newly washed and dried sweater. She always added the piece of jewelry to the hanger that she thought went best with the item of clothing. Landry caressed the pearls lightly and had to brush back tears.

"I sure do miss you, Aunt Tildie. Being back here after being gone for so long just makes me miss you being here more."

She put the clothes on the back of the closet and went back and found a cute pair of ballerina slippers that were the same cream color that was in the skirt. She was set for tonight.

She usually wore boots with most of her outfits. Ankle boots, knee boots, rain boots, it really didn't matter. She even wore them with dresses, though jeans were her go to favorite. She had always loved boots for some reason. She would be glad to get all of her boots when they delivered her things from Bent Branch.

The next three hours were spent at the bookstore with Ms. Millie. Landry learned a lot during that time. Ms. Millie was wonderful. She showed Landry the back office and explained how she did the ordering. Landry found out that it was very similar to the way she had ordered books for the library.

Ms. Millie was in charge of much more than she had let on. She kept up with inventory, did the bank deposit each day after she left work and took care of any problems that might arise. She was well versed on how the bookstore ran and she cared about it like it was her own.

As she told Landry, "Tildie and I were friends for many, many years. I was the first person she met when she moved here from Bent Branch. On weekends when I didn't have to work in the school cafeteria, I would go out to the farm and help her shell beans, scrape corn, cut okra and all that stuff. Then, we would spend a whole day canning the things she harvested. Oh, she always made sure I had plenty to carry back home with me for my family, which my late husband loved. But, you know what? The talkin' we did and the fellowship we had while we did those chores are some of the best times of my life. Why, I felt like Tildie and I were sisters. We had nicknames for each other, too. Oh, everybody else called us 'Mil and Til' but we called each other 'Ebony and Ivory' but SHE was Ebony and I was Ivory." People would look a little shocked when we called each other that in public. Then, we would walk away laughing and hanging on to each other. I sure do miss Tildie. More than anybody knows. She was there for me when my husband, Clive, went to be with the Lord. I had a hard time with that. We were married a long time and our daughter, Rose, had already married and moved away. I don't think I would have made it without Tildie during those sad times."

Ms. Millie continued, "So you see, Landry, when I retired and Tildie needed help with this place, I didn't bat an eye. I promised her that I would look after it and work it just like it was my own. I meant that. I will do the same for you. She loved you very much, you know. Talked about her 'little Lan' all the time. She was so proud that you became a librarian like her. She loved her part time job at the library downtown and said she wished she would have been full time, but the work at the farm had to come first since that was the bulk of her income. Then, when she bought the bookstore and apartment building, those took up all of her time. When she found out she had cancer and had to have treatments for it, Lisa and I stepped in and helped to take most of the responsibility off her."

Millie looked sad as she continued, "The treatments were hard on her, Landry. Ravaged her body. She pretty much stayed in the apartment and went out on the balcony when she wanted some fresh air. She had a nurse come in every day to take her vitals and check on her. Lisa made sure she had meals delivered, even though for a while Tildie survived on protein shakes and yogurt. That was about all she could tolerate with the effects of the treatments. They worked, though and about 8 months before she passed, they told her the cancer was gone."

"What happened, Ms. Millie? It seems the cancer came back in full force." Landry questioned.

"I'm not sure, Landry. Tildie came back from her recheck about two months before she passed and said the scans they took a few weeks before the appointment showed that it was back. She had been so very sick during the first go round with those treatments and she said she was not going through it again; that her body just was not strong enough. She thought that she would have more time and had even talked about going to visit you and Bent Branch. She passed away just two months later. She had made arrangements with the local funeral home that said she did not want a funeral service, memorial service or anything of that nature. She wanted to be cremated and her ashes scattered out at the farm with no fanfare. She put all this in writing with Adam. He is the one who carried out her wishes."

"I know when he called to notify my Mom that Aunt Tildie had died, he said that there wouldn't be a funeral due to Aunt Tildie's wishes. I am glad that it was him that put her ashes at the farm. I can tell he really thought a lot of her."

"Honey chile, he loved Tildie. And, she loved him. They got real close those summers he worked at the farm when he was in high school. She told me in confidence that he was the closest to a son that she would ever have. She also told me about the times he went to check on her when she was sick. He is the one who arranged for the nurse to go by and check on her. I pick on the man, but I am thankful for his care of Tildie. He will always be special to me. Don't tell him that, though. I don't want my reputation for being ornery to fade." She smiled.

"Ms. Millie. This time today has meant so much to me. I remember you being at the farm when I was young. I didn't even connect that it was you that saved me from that bull that day until I was thinking about the farm in bed last night. You saved my life. I also remember Aunt Tildie telling me that you were her sister. I never questioned it. Later, I remember me saying something to my Mom about her two sisters. She said she just had one sister, Tildie. That's when I realized that you and Aunt Tildie were God Given sisters, not biological ones."

"I like that description, Landry. That is exactly what we were. And, I am glad I was there when that mean old bull charged you. Scared me to live right seeing you come that close to death as a child. But, just remember, I still got my eye on you. I don't want to hear about any foolishness. It's bad enough that you found a body and blessed out the Mayor the first week you are in town. If I didn't know better, I would think you did have a little of my blood in ya." Ms. Millie laughed.

"Word sure does get around in a little town.," Landry smiled. "I will try to stay out of trouble. Right now, I have to get ready to go to dinner. Adam is taking me out to eat tonight. I am hoping to meet a few more of the locals."

"Behave yourself, Landry. Adam is one of the finest boys I have ever known. I have no doubt that he will be a wonderful friend to you. Maybe even more, if the Lord sees fit." She winked and Landry rolled her eyes and got up to leave.

As she was leaving Jasmine Bloom Books, Maisy and Jenna were walking in the door. She heard Ms. Millie giving them heck for being late and the girls said they were sorry. "Yep," she said to herself, "I think Ms. Millie has it all under control here."

Landry walked back in the lobby of Magnolia Place. Lisa waved at her and called her in her office. "They delivered the rest of your things today. I got them to put the square metal thingee at the back of the grill area on the grass there. When you have time to supervise, I will get our maintenance guys to bring it all up to your apartment."

"Wonderful," Landry replied. "I am actually going out to dinner tonight but, how about tomorrow? I will let you know when they can start. Thank you so much Lisa."

"Sounds good. I also wanted to ask you if you noticed the little single button beside your intercom buzzer in your apartment?"

"I have. What is it for?" Landry asked.

"The last doorman locks the front door in the lobby when he leaves his shift. The residents all have a pass key if they come in after the doorman is gone. If it is late at night and you have someone coming to visit, they can call you on their cell when they are here and you can push that little button to open the lobby door for them. When they close it, it automatically locks back. Miss Tildie had that installed when she became ill in case she had to call for an ambulance after hours."

"Thanks for letting me know, although I usually go to bed at a decent hour so, hopefully, I won't have to use it." Landry replied.

"And, because I am nosey, just who are you going to dinner with tonight?" Lisa smiled.

"That would be your cousin." Landry smiled back and went to the elevator.

She went to her apartment and made a fresh pot of coffee. While it was brewing, she jumped in the shower. When she got out, she put on her thick terry cloth robe and put her hair in a towel for the time being. She went back to the kitchen, grabbed a cup of coffee and some yogurt to hold her over until dinner. Then, she went out on the balcony to eat her yogurt and think.

Fred's murder was always on the edge of her mind. It bugged her that the Sheriff had no leads on who could have done it. It made her anxious when she thought about it happening in the building. She also thought about Fred's sister, Melodie. She remembered someone saying that Melodie was out of town a lot, but wondered if they had contacted her to give her the news about her brother. Adam had said that Fred's folks were both deceased and that Fred lived in an old trailer that they had owned on the outskirts of town. She guessed that Wyatt and his deputies had questioned the neighbors there.

She had finished her yogurt and drank her cup of coffee. She got up, went back inside and poured herself another cup to take to the bedroom to drink while she was getting ready.

She was ready and sitting in the living room waiting for Adam to arrive. She looked at the things from her car and decided that she needed to get those put up tonight before all of her other things were brought up. She would be glad to get her things back, especially her clothes. She hoped she wasn't overdressed for dinner. Adam said this place was called 'Sky High Tavern'. She had no idea what it was like but, hopefully she would fit in.

Adam arrived and walked her to his car. The ride over was pleasant and she even recognized a few of the older shops on the way out of town. A rabbit ran out in front of them; thankfully, it was far enough away that Adam could stop the car and let it get out of the way. The rabbit got to the other side of the road and turned back and Landry swore that it smiled at them. They laughed and drove on to the restaurant, talking about the murder and how they hoped it was solved soon.

When they got there, Adam opened her door for her and they walked up to a very small building. Adam stopped to say something to a young man there and they kept walking. They stopped and her mouth flew open. There in front of her was a chair lift.

"What on earth? Adam, I thought you said we were going to dinner."

"We are. Remember I told you this place was called the 'Sky High Tavern'? Well, the only way to get to it is by riding the chair lift. The tavern is on the top of that mountain." He pointed.

Landry was stunned. Who had ever heard of such a thing? Oh, well, if this was the way to the food, she was game.

The operator of the chair lift lifted the railing for them and they backed up to sit down. He slammed the rail closed and gave them a push. Off they were flying through the sky to go eat dinner.

"What a novel idea. What do the owners do when it is raining, snowing, icy or bad weather?" She looked at Adam.

"In that case, the tavern is closed. See, the people who own and run it are millionaires many times over. They made their money in Hollywood and then decided they wanted to live life peacefully and on their own terms. They found Bobwhite Mountain, fell in love with it and decided to open this place. This used to be a tourist attraction and had a few rides and some live shows and food available at the top of the mountain. That closed down years ago and Brad and Lucy Pugh, the owners of the tavern, bought the property and created something unique for the town. They love chatting with customers, providing employment for locals...with great pay, I might add... and they also have aspiring singers from town to provide some entertainment for diners. Pretty cool, huh?"

"Very cool." Landry replied.

"The name of the smaller mountain that we are riding up is named 'Sky High Mountain.' When the Pugh's opened their tavern, they named it after the mountain. That and, of course, it is in the sky." He looked at her and asked, "Have you ever been on a chair lift before?"

"Nope. I love it, though. Slowly riding up the side of a mountain is amazing."

"Well," Adam explained to her, "when we get to the top, a person will grab ahold of our chair and raise the bar. Then, we just gently jump out and the chair circles around to go back down the mountain."

"That sounds simple enough," Landry whispered as she was taking in all of the awesome views.

Sure enough, they got to the top and the young man working the chair lift lifted the rail for them. Adam jumped out expertly and turned around to take Landry's hand. Only, Landry was yelling something. She was saying that something was stuck.

"My skirt is wrapped around the bottom of the chair. I can't…" About that time, the chair started circling around the track to go back down the mountain.

The worker panicked and shouted, "Put the rail down ma'am." Landry was yelling and saying something neither the worker or Adam could understand.

The worker shouted again, "Put the rail down or you will fall out, ma'am."

Landry clamped the rail shut. The worker held up his walkie talkie.

"I will call down to the bottom and let them know what is happening. Once you get there, they will stop the chair lift and get your skirt untangled."

Adam was running after the chair until the worker pulled him back and told him he would fall if he kept it up.

Adam yelled to Landry, "Stay calm and they will help you at the bottom. Twist your ring."

The worker looked at Adam strangely and Adam walked far enough away that others wouldn't knock him down when they exited the chairs. He felt awful about all of this.

Chapter 8

"Well this is a fine mess." Landry said aloud to herself. "How embarrassing. By now, Adam must think I am a complete fool."

She sighed and started looking at the views again. It really was a gorgeous sight. It was a little cool, but felt good to her since she could feel her face and it was hot. She knew it had to be blood red by now. At least she wasn't having a panic attack. Things like this were always happening to her, so she was used to it, sadly. She got to the bottom and saw the young man working the chair lift. He looked very serious. He grabbed her chair, then flipped a switch.

"Just a sec, Ma'am and I will get you fixed right up."

He then hit another switch and announced on a speaker that could be heard two counties away to all of the people going up the mountain.

"Don't panic, folks. I had to stop the lift so that I can get this here lady's skirt untangled. Won't be but just a minute and we will have you moving again."

"Oh. My. Lanta." Landry said under her breath. Could he have yelled that any louder over the speaker?

He pulled the rail up and reached down to get her skirt out of whatever it was stuck on. He finally got up and handed her the bottom of the skirt.

"There ya are. Sorry, but it got a little grease on it. At least I got it out without tearing it, though. Now, if I were you, I would take the bottom of the skirt and gather it all up and shove it between your legs to hold it in. Don't want that to happen again."

Landry heard giggling and snickering. It seems her helpful worker had forgotten to turn off the speaker and had shouted to everyone and his brother that she should shove her skirt between her legs.

"Oh for goodness sake." Landry said and then stood up and did exactly what the worker had suggested. She pulled the skirt down to just below her knees and sat on the rest of it. THIS ought to be a good look for Adam to see when she finally got back to the top.

She thanked the man for his help and he clamped the rail back in place on the chair. She started her second ride up the Mountain. The nice folks on their way down all yelled at her and said they were glad she got her skirt untangled. Could this night get any worse?

Apparently, it could.

When she got to the top, the worker grabbed her chair and made sure to hold it with all his might this time. He raised the rail and Landry jumped out, trying to hold onto her skirt that was still between her legs and underneath her. She got out but as soon as her feet hit the ground, her tender ankle gave out and she fell. Right into Adam's chest. It surprised him and they both fell flat on the ground. He jumped up fast and reached down to help Landry up.

She looked up at him and said, "Adam, I told yo…"

He cut her off and said, "Landry, you are not a jinx. Stop saying that. I will admit you may be a little clumsy, but it makes things interesting."

She looked at him for a second and they both burst out laughing and brushed themselves off.

As they approached the tavern, Landry decided it was worth the effort to get here. It reminded her of the little restaurants in Helen, GA that she had visited with Aunt Tildie and the Ladies Group from the church when she was little. It was a charming place.

They walked up a path that was lit with tall lanterns and went inside. The inside was just as wonderful as the outside.

Adam told the doorman that he and Landry would like to visit the restroom before they sat down and that he had a reservation. They went to freshen up and Landry tried to fix the flyaways of her hair. Between the chair lift and all of her twisting and turning because of her skirt, she had quite a few. Thank goodness she had gone with a bun tonight so she just had to redo that while she was in front of the mirror. She met Adam back in the lobby and their waiter took them to their table. He asked if they wanted to start with a drink.They both asked for sweet iced tea at the same time. He nodded and gave them their menus.

They were looking over everything on the menu when Landry excitedly said, "Oh, they have one of my favorites."

Adam looked up, "Yeah? What's that?"

She told him, "Crabmeat Au Gratin." I love it but hardly ever have it. What are you getting?"

Adam put his menu down and looked at her and winked.

"Steak. That's what I always get here. Their steaks are so tender and they cook them just right."

Landry looked at him questionably, "Come here often, do you?"

"Not really. They do have the best food around but, most nights I order out and have it delivered to my office. I usually spend half the night there since I have client meetings during the day. I need peace and quiet to focus on Wills, Estates and the like. It's just easier for me to eat at the office unless I have a business dinner scheduled. Sometimes, I do go to the B&B and have dinner with Mom."

The waiter came back at that moment to bring their drinks and get their orders. When he left, a light came on above the stage in front and a young woman with long, brown, straight hair came out. Her outfit reminded Landry of 70's attire. She had on a long skirt, knee high boots and layered tops. They were all lacey and flowing. She had a voice that was low and lyrical. Adam and Landry sat and listened until their food was delivered.

Landry had ordered a salad with her entree and the fresh bread was amazing. "You are absolutely right, Adam. This is a great place. The food was wonderful."

After they finished eating and talking, Adam was raising his hand to ask for the check when the front door flew open. A woman with wiry, bleached blonde hair ran in. She was short and had on jeans and a leather jacket. She was yelling something that Landry didn't understand at first.

"Where is she? Where is that murderer? Ah-ha…there you are."

She went tearing off towards the stage where the woman who had been singing was walking very fast to the exit door.

"Portia. Portia Roy. I know you either killed my brother or know who did. You stop right there you little tramp."

Portia whirled around and said, "You have some gall calling anybody a tramp, Melodie. Isn't that like that old saying, 'the pot calling the kettle black'? You stay away from me. I mean it." She went running through the door.

Two men from the restaurant staff grabbed Melodie before she could follow Portia and escorted her outside and into the chair lift. They called the people on the ground below and told them to get security ready to get Melodie off the property.

"I take it that was Fred's sister, Melodie." Landry said.

"Yup. That would be her." Adam shook his head as he stood up and went to the back of Landry's chair..

"I am going to have some questions for you when we get down off this Mountain, Attorney Wilcox." Landry said as she stood up. "I am sure you will, Miss Burke." Adam asked for the check.

They exited the chair lift at the bottom with no "wardrobe malfunctions" on Landry's part. As they started the drive home Adam spoke first, "We have about a 30 minute drive, so ask all the questions you want."

"Ok," Landry started. "First of all, I know several

people have said that Melodie works out of town and is gone much of the time. What kind of job does she have that she travels so much?"

Adam cleared his throat, "Well, Melodie tells everybody that is the road manager for a band."

"I hear a 'but' coming." Landry replied.

"Yeah, well, she is actually a groupie for several throwback rock bands." He waited for Landry's response.

"A groupie? Well, that is the last thing I was expecting you to say. She can't make enough money to survive on that."

Adam said, "Landry, she goes with these bands on the road. They do pay her…in cash. You see," Adam wondered if he looked as uncomfortable as he felt at this moment. "She performs…services…for the band members and they pay her."

Landry looked confused, "What kinds of servi…Oh. gross."

Adam nodded his head really fast. "Yes, I feel the same way but, you wanted to know. I only found out the truth because one of my associates was representing a band member in another matter and he told him about it. How she can have such low self esteem I will never understand."

"I wonder why she was accusing Portia of killing him? Everybody has told me that Fred was this quiet, unassuming guy who didn't talk much. Maybe he and Portia were friends."

"Not sure about that but, I will tell you that I have always felt something was a little off with Fred's persona. I mean, maybe he had a life that none of us knew about. It's true that he didn't talk much so I guess we wouldn't have known what he did outside of work or when we weren't around him. That's really kinda sad. Anyway, I saw him a couple of times when I was on the road out to the farm and." Landry interrupted him.

"Wait, do you mean Aunt Tildie's old farm?"

"Well, yeah I was out there a lot when she owned it. I worked there during the summers when I was in high school. Doing some chores around the place and stuff."

"Ms. Millie mentioned to me that you did." Landry informed him.

"But, I also go out there a good bit since my Aunt and Uncle bought it."

"Lisa's folks? How did I not know they had bought Aunt Tildie's farm? This town is like putting together a puzzle." She giggled.

"I guess I thought Lisa would have told you. Sorry I didn't mention it. I will be glad to take you out there when things settle down for you to meet them and look around the farm and see what has been done in the years since you've been gone."

"That sounds great. I would love that. Now, go on with your story of seeing Fred on the road."

"I saw him two different times…once in a beat up old truck without a tailgate. He had a man in the truck and, let's just say, the man looked a little sketchy to me. I mean, I have friends of all types and don't judge, it's just that this guy looked mad at the world and kinda greasy. While I was behind them, he kept looking back behind the seat in the truck like he was keeping an eye on something."

Adam turned off of the main road and onto the road they would take straight into Bobwhite Mountain while Landry listened intently to what he was saying. "The second time was even weirder to me. He was driving the same truck but he had a different passenger that time. Looked like a thin female to me. She had one of those hoodies on with the hood over her head. All I could see was a little of her blonde hair that was escaping the hoodie and flying in the wind from the cracked window. She kept her head down the entire time."

"Wonder if it was Melodie? She has blonde hair." Landry guessed.

"No, it was definitely not Melodie. I could tell that this woman was tall…much taller than Melodie. Probably nothing but, both times Fred avoided looking at me. I mean, the first time I could understand since I was behind him and just tapped my horn as I turned off the road to head to the farm; but, the second time we were on the double lane road and I was right beside him."

They turned onto Main Street and pulled into the parking garage using Landry's key card. "I'll just walk you up. It will make me feel better to see you go into your apartment and lock it behind you. All this talk about Fred has me worried about who got in this building and killed him." He parked next to Landry's Bug in the other spot designated for her apartment.

They got to her apartment door and he said, "I had a

great time tonight, Landry. Well, except for your skirt mishap and Melodie barging in the tavern and creating havoc. Actually, even during those things going on, I still enjoyed your company."

"So did I, Adam. The food was delicious and I agree that the company was superb. Thank you so much for inviting me. Next time, it will be my treat."

"Nope, for two reasons. One: You need to save all the money you can so that you can show those profits after the year is up. I want to see you be a success. Two: I am an old fashioned kind of guy. If I take a girl out, I pay. Plus, I am a single attorney. I think I can splurge for a few meals for us." He laughed.

"That is very admirable of you. But, I do love to cook. As soon as I get things organized and in a routine, I will cook for you. I hate cooking for just myself, so it will work for both of us."

"That sounds like a plan. Night, Landry. Lock up when I leave, please."

"No worries…goodnight Adam." Landry opened her door and went in, turning around to lock it and put the chain on. Ms. Millie was right; Adam was really a nice guy. She started to take a step and felt something under her foot. She bent over and picked up a note that was folded over. "Probably something Lisa wanted me to know so she shoved it under my door after I left," Landry thought. She took off her shoes as she went across the room and sat on the love seat. She opened the note and gasped. Someone had typed up a very short note:

LEAVE IT ALONE. YOU DON'T WANT TO BE
MIXED UP IN IT

Landry stared at the note. She contemplated calling
Adam to come back but decided against it. She would take
the note to Wyatt tomorrow at the Sheriff's Department and
then tell Adam about it. This was scaring her now.
Someone was stalking her building, killing an employee
and now threatening her. She had to find out who it was
and soon.

Chapter 9

The next few weeks went by in a blur. Landry had the meet and greet with the residents of Magnolia Place. All were in attendance except for the semi resident Author , Karen Scott (she left for home before the meeting started, but stopped by Landry's apartment on her way out, introduced herself and explained there was an emergency in her family and that she had to leave for the time being.) and Cody and Larissa Collins who were out of town for a race. The meeting went well and Landry had ordered some finger foods and snacks so that everyone would linger and mingle with each other. She provided them all with her cell number if they ever needed her. After the meeting, Landry talked to the security company worker, Glen Mayhew, who rented the third apartment on her floor about installing cameras in the building. He said that he would work something up and bring it to her so that she could present it to her accountant for approval.

She also spent a few hours each day at the bookstore learning the ropes and doing some things she wanted to improve on. Ms. Millie always tried to shoo her out quickly but Landry had learned how to put her foot down and they actually worked very nicely together. Ms. Millie was a treasure trove of information for Landry and she loved the time she spent with her. Ms. Millie really did remind Landry of Aunt Tildie so much.

She had taken the note to Wyatt at the Sheriff's office

the day after she found it. He took it for processing and told her they still had no leads. That didn't sit well with her. She had met the residents of the building and some of them had children. Some of the wives stayed home or worked only part time. There were others still that were elderly. She wanted to be sure they were all safe in her building. The note also made her very nervous. Who would even think that she was asking questions about Fred's death? She had just gotten into town the day he was murdered. Who was watching her and felt threatened by her?

A new doorman had been hired to replace Fred and they had really lucked out in that department. Josh Henley was a recently retired police officer from the next town over. After he was home for only a month, his wife informed him that he needed to get another job because she was used to having some time by herself. He was working Fred's old hours of 1pm until 11pm. That worked out great since it gave his wife time in the afternoon to be by herself, but he was home before midnight so that she wasn't alone during the night. He was a stocky man with a bald head who was a stickler for rules, which meant that he and Garrett got along wonderfully.

They still hadn't filled the part time doorman position that ran from 11pm until 4am. Landry still was adamant that she wanted someone in the lobby 24/7. Lisa had told her this morning that they had an excellent prospect coming to interview for the job today. Zack Williams was a 26 year old computer programmer who worked from home. He and his wife, Mora, had been married just 6 months. They lived with Zack's Mom who was widowed and Mora was still in college getting her Master's Degree in Social Work. He had called Lisa about the job after his Mom had seen a flier in the window of Magnolia Place. He sounded promising.

She had also been to church with Adam. He and his Mom attended the same church as Aunt Tildie had attended and Landry had joined the Ladies Club there already. She had such fond memories of Aunt Tildie including her as a child when the Ladies Club had different events. Now, she was an adult and looked forward to the fellowship this Club afforded her. She had already met a few of the ladies around her age and was excited to make new friends.

Landry had finally gotten all of her things put up in the apartment. It was a nice combination of cozy and elegant with some of Aunt Tildie's things mixed in with hers. This morning, she had gone to the big box store outside of town and bought several items she needed like a new vacuum cleaner after the old one broke, new toiletries and hair products and a new shower curtain and rugs for her bathroom. She also bought a huge bottle of laundry detergent, clothes softener, dryer sheets and two new laundry baskets while she was there. Each apartment at Magnolia Place had washer and dryer hookups in them. No communal laundry room for the residents. She loaded all that up and drove to the grocery store on Main Street in Bobwhite Mountain. Greene's Groceries. It was right down from Magnolia Place and she loved to shop local when possible. Lisa had told her that Lester and Grace Waters owned the store. Grace had been a Greene before she married Lester and he liked the idea of keeping her family name on the store when she inherited it. There, Landry stocked up on food. Meat, veggies, fruits, cereal, milk, yogurt, the ketchup chips that she loved and all sorts of things. She was determined to stock her kitchen and cook dinner at home more often. She loved to cook so much and Aunt Tildie made sure that she knew how to cook old fashioned, southern food.

She put it all in her little car and went back home. She grabbed a cart from the corral in the garage and loaded it up and then went upstairs and unloaded it. She made one more trip to get the things she couldn't get in the cart the first go round and dropped those off at the apartment and took her cart back to the corral in the garage. She stood there and put her hands on her hips. "I sure hope I am as innovative as Aunt Tildie was. What a great idea she had to do this."

After she took off her shoes and grabbed a diet drink from the fridge, she sat down before starting dinner for tonight. She was going to put some chicken, canned soup, boxed dressing and a can of green beans in the crockpot before she left to go see Ms. Millie at the bookstore. She had a couple of things to talk to her about. She sent Adam a message and asked if he wanted to have dinner at her apartment tonight. They had been spending most nights doing things together unless he was swamped at work. He replied back that it would be wonderful to have a home cooked meal.

She had gotten some homemade cranberry salad from the deli and some fresh baked bread that she would serve with the meal. She had also picked up fresh strawberries, heavy cream and a half of a pound cake. She would get all that ready when she got back from the bookstore and they could have strawberry shortcake and coffee for dessert.

She threw the ingredients in the crockpot, turned it on low and dialed Wyatt's number on her phone. "Yup." he yelled when he picked up the call.

"Hello, Sheriff. This is Landry…" He stopped her and said, "Please call me Wyatt, Landry. Now that I know you aren't a criminal or anything."

"Ha-Ha," she said sarcastically. "Wyatt, have you made any progress on Fred's murder? I have a few questions about things that I have been wondering about that might help you out depending on the answers."

Wyatt sighed very loudly. "Landry, I am asking you to please stay out of this. We are actively working this murder investigation and it is a stop priority, believe me. I will let you know when we find out who did this. Try to stop worrying about all this…I know you must have hundreds of things to straighten out at the building and the bookstore." Landry noticed that he didn't even acknowledge her statement about her having questions about some things.

"I cannot stop worrying about it. It happened in a building I own that also happens to be my home. I worry about it, not just for me, but for the residents of my building. I don't want whoever it was that killed Fred come back here and hurt somebody else. You saw that note I brought you that was shoved under my door. Obviously, whoever the murderer is, he/she has been back to the scene at least once…to deliver that threatening note."

Wyatt sighed again, "I do understand that, Landry. Just please be very careful and if you get any more notes or find anything that you think would be helpful to the investigation, bring it to me. Personally, I wish that Miss Tildie had installed security cameras in the building."

"That is something I am going to do as soon as I can." Landry replied.

She heard a loud buzz and Wyatt said he had to go now. He had a meeting in 5 minutes and that was the front desk reminding him. "Just be careful, Landry, since we don't know who left that note yet." He hung up the phone.

She decided she was hungry and walked into the kitchen. She started the coffee maker. Then, she whipped up a couple of eggs and made her some french toast. She got the ketchup and put a big slug of it on her plate. Everyone always laughed that she ate ketchup on her french toast but she didn't like it sweet with syrup. She walked out on the balcony to eat her breakfast. She took every chance she got to sit out there and marvel at the wonderful views.

Once she was done, she put on some jeans and a crisp, new white t-shirt. She added a thin, light blue cardigan for the time being since it was still a little cool out. She knew that it would warm up nicely this afternoon, though. She wore her white sneakers and pulled her unruly hair up with a scarf. On the way out of the building, she said good morning to Lisa and Garrett.

"Good morning, Landry. Hope you have a wonderful

day today. The weather is supposed to be gorgeous." Lisa smiled.

"Good morning, Miss Burke." Garrett said in his stoic voice. "Have a pleasant day."

Landry smiled as she left the building and headed over to the bookstore. Garrett was such a throwback to a more formal time. It was actually kind of nice to listen to him talk in such a regal way. No wonder her Aunt had hired him, she laughed.

She stepped into the bookstore and, like always, took in a deep breath of apple cinnamon spice and new book scent. She loved it so much. She heard Ms. Millie singing in the back room and then heard her yell, "Hold your horses, I will be right with ya."

Landry laughed and waited for her to come out from the back. Ms. Millie saw that it was her and said, "Darn, I thought I was about to get a big sale."

"Nope. Just me. I have a few things I want to run by you. Two are ideas for the bookstore and another is a favor I want to ask of you." Landry replied.

"Well, start with the ideas for the bookstore first so I can go ahead and shoot them down if they are lame." Ms. Millie smiled and Landry knew she was joking. She had finally gotten used to Ms. Millie's sense of humor.

"I was sitting on a bench in the park the other day and I saw a pretty large group of young mothers there with toddlers. I went over to them to introduce myself and found out that they actually get together two or three days a week to let the kids play together and get out of the house. They are all stay at home Moms who need to talk to adults every now and then and also get their kids out of the house and let them socialize with other kids. Here's what I was thinking.

What if we took that small storage room in the back and made it a small room just for children. We could put some lower shelves with books appropriate for their age in there. I could put down some carpet and a rug to make it safe for them. Maybe even set up an area to have movie time one day a week. Another day a week, we could set aside an hour to read a children's book to them and then let them talk about it amongst themselves. I would love to do that with them and keep them here for an hour so that their Moms could run to the diner or somewhere else and grab some coffee and chat. It would give them a break. On the day we have movie time, I could make a simple snack and have some juice. We will have the parents fill out a form with any allergies the children might have. We could make sure that the movie has a coordinating book and, if we plan them in advance, we can be sure to have enough books in case the parents want to purchase one. We have plenty of extra storage in the big room, so I think we can make it work. I realize that the library has a children's area but doing this here would be another option for them. What do you think?" Landry looked at Ms. Millie for her opinion.

"That sounds like a pretty good idea. As long as it is understood that you will be the one here on those days. I have paid my dues dealing with kids of all ages. I don't want to have to babysit, even if it is for just an hour at a time." Ms. Millie made her point clear.

Landry smiled, "Perfect. I want to do this. When I was the librarian in my hometown, I loved going over to the children's area and hanging out with them and the Children's Librarian. I would enjoy doing that here. If you want to research and see which popular children's books have been made into movies, we can make a schedule of which movies we will show and be sure to order the books in case anyone wants to purchase them. I will choose some of my favorites to read to them on the other day. Let's try to make the movie day on Mondays around 11 and the reading on Thursdays at the same time. That way, the Moms can go sit down and relax somewhere before the heavy lunch crowd gathers. I will get Lisa to put me in touch with someone to carpet the room and put a fresh coat of paint in there. I'm sure I can get our maintenance guys from the building to move what little stuff we have stored in there to the big storage room."

Landry snapped her fingers, "I will also go to the thrift store and see if I can find some children's tables and chairs and a few toys to put in there. I will mention to the Moms that start bringing their kids here to always think of us when they go to clean out their children's toys. That should help us replace any that get broken or old."

"Seems like you got this all figured out." Ms. Millie smiled. "What was the other thing you wanted to talk to me about for the bookstore?"

Landry reached in her purse and pulled out a bright colored paper. "I had Lisa make up this flier for us. We will put it in the front window. This won't begin until the Fall, so that we will have time to order and receive the books. I am going to start up a Book Club here at the bookstore. Customers can sign up on the list and once we see how many are interested, we will all read the same book every month. We can order a copy for everyone in the Book Club. On the last Tuesday of the month, we will gather here after hours and discuss the book. We can have coffee, tea and maybe some pastries." Landry looked thrilled with her idea and looked at Ms. Millie for her reaction.

Ms. Millie nodded her head and said, "I actually love that idea. I mentioned that to Tildie right before she got sick and we were going to do something like this. After she started her treatments, it was put on hold. Let's do it. Now, what else did you want to talk to me about?"

Landry sighed and said, "Ms. Millie. this murder in my building has to be solved soon. I have people that live there coming to me and they are worried the killer is going to come back. Now, I feel like it is an isolated event but, I have to say I am worried about it. This is confidential information. Only the Sheriff's Office, Adam and I know about this. I got a note slipped under my door telling me to leave it alone. That I didn't want to be involved in this."

"What?" Ms. Millie shouted. "You were threatened? Oh no, that just won't do. Wyatt has to get off his butt and find the person who did this and is trying to scare you. I won't have this happening to Tildie's niece. Let me get right down to that Sheriff's office and have a come to Jesus moment with Wyatt Collins." She went to grab her purse.

"No, Ms. Millie, you can't do that. First of all, you aren't even supposed to know about the note. And Wyatt and his deputies are working on the case. I am sure they are just as frustrated as we are and will be glad to find this killer. What I came to ask you is if you would go with me somewhere to talk to somebody about this."

Ms. Millie put her purse back down. "Just where and who are you talking about?"

"The other night when Adam and I were at the Sky High, Fred's sister, Melodie, came in and…"

"Humph. that one. She has been up to no good since she was in middle school. I even tried to mentor her in high school before she dropped out and took off with some band. I really don't even want to be in close range to her. No tellin' what kinds of diseases that girl is carrying."

"Now, Ms. Millie. I know about her shady ways, but what I was getting at was that she confronted the singer at the Sky High, Portia. She called Portia a tramp and said that she knew Portia was responsible for Fred's murder, or at least knew who was. I want to go out to Fred's trailer and just see if Melodie is there. I want to ask her what she meant by that. Will you come with me since I have no idea where the trailer is and I know you know everything about this town?"

Ms. Millie stared at Landry for what seemed like minutes. When she finally spoke, she said, "I guess I will have to come with you since if I let you go alone, Tildie would come to haunt me tonight. We will have to wait until the girls get here around 3:30, though. Don't want to lose any sales just to go galavanting around on a hunch."

"Thank you. I will pull up outside around 3:30 to pick you up." She hugged Ms. Milie and said, "You are the best."

Ms. Millie responded with, "Mmm hmm. The best at gettin' sucked into shenanigans like this."

Landry laughed and headed out to go meet with her accountant before she headed back to her apartment.

She walked down two blocks and turned right on Cannon Street. Her accountant's office was on the ground floor of a red brick building. She went in and told the receptionist that she was there to see Mr. Harcourt. She didn't even have time to sit down before he was walking towards her with his hand out. She shook it and introduced herself. I am so happy to meet you, Miss Burke. We have a lot to discuss. "A lot?," Landry thought to herself but didn't say aloud. She thought she was here to sign some papers and be on her way.

"Please sit down." Mr. Harcourt said as they walked in the room. "Would you like some coffee or something else to drink?"

"I would love a coffee, thank you." Landry realized she was very thirsty and welcomed the caffeine boost.

He buzzed his assistant and then got down to business. "Miss Burke, as you know, the Will states that you have to make a profit on both properties that Miss Tildie left you by the end of the first year in order to officially inherit them. The clock is already ticking on that and I have a few suggestions to make to help you reach that goal."

"What would those be, Mr. Harcourt?"

"First of all, and I approached this subject with your Aunt before she passed away, do you think you really need three doormen? This is an apartment building you are running, not a hotel. I am sure the residents there can get themselves in and out of the door without help."

Landry, for some reason, felt a wave of protection. For her residents, sure, but mostly for her employees and herself. This man acted as if she were a complete idiot. She decided to play his little game.

"And, what did my Aunt have to say about this, Mr. Harcourt?"

He looked a little flustered and reluctantly said, "Well, she thought that because she offered these doormen in the lobby that it justified charging higher rent on the apartments. Something about the residents there feeling safer. Of course, that was before this murder took place on your first day in town. Not to mention that it was the murder of one of the very doormen that are supposed to be in the lobby at all times."

His assistant brought in Landry's coffee and she took a huge gulp of it before she spoke. "Mr. Harcourt, I completely agree with my Aunt. The added convenience of doormen…or, as I think of them, lobby assistants, being there around the clock IS comforting to our residents. What you might not know is that they have other duties to perform other than opening doors. That is an antiquated term and I realize that most places don't have 'doormen' anymore but the position is still needed. My lobby assistants are very valuable to the building and yes, I also agree that it justifies the higher rent. Magnolia Place is known as an upscale apartment building and that title is due to the 'extras' that we provide. So, you see, this is a mute point and I won't budge on it. On to the next issue, Mr. Harcourt."

He cleared his throat and looked a little put out. "Yes, well the other thing is that your Aunt spent an exorbitant amount on paintings for the Event Room. I have spoken to our local art gallery director and you could recoup what she paid for most of those paintings and even make a nice profit if you decide to sell them. Now, I…"

"That is a non-starter, Mr. Harcourt. My Aunt entrusted me with her most precious possessions. I will not sell them just to show a profit. What I will do is work very hard to keep the apartments rented, use common sense when considering expenditures and make sure that the bookstore makes a profit as well. You see, Mr. Harcourt, I do value your opinion and I hope that you will work with me to keep all of the accounts soluble. My Aunt trusted you and therefore, I know you have to be one of the best in your field. You should understand that I am also extremely well versed on budgets and making profits. I was a Librarian before I left that position to come here and I was in charge of many employees. I was also the person who was held responsible for any decisions that were made there, financial or otherwise. Are we done for today? I have other places to be. If you have any more papers I need to sign other than the ones I signed in Mr. Wilcox's office, please forward them to Magnolia Place's manager, Lisa, and she will present them to me." Landry stood to leave.

"Very well, Miss Burke. I believe all of the paperwork is signed. If you need my assistance further, please call to make an appointment."

Landy turned and walked out the door. When she got back on the sidewalk, she started shaking. This always happens. She was cool and calm in situations of this sort until after it was over. What was it with some of the men in this town? Did Mr. Harcourt really think she would cower down to him and do what she was certain was against what Aunt Tildie wanted? No matter…she had other things to accomplish today.

First up, she went to the K&L Diner and grabbed an iced coffee and a bagel to go. She then walked to the park and sat on a bench to eat her snack. She noticed the young mothers group again and waited until she was done eating her bagel to approach them. She told them about the plan at the bookstore for the Children's Room. They loved the idea and said to please let them know when the room was ready for them. Landry promised that she would and left to make a quick stop at the apartment building before it was time to pick up Ms. Millie for their trip to see if Melodie was in town and at Fred's trailer.

When she walked in the door of the building, Lisa looked at her like she was very relieved to see her. "What's up, Lisa?" Landry smiled. "Landry, this is Mrs. Barbara Cartwright; the mayor's wife. She was just telling me that she would like to cancel the event for the local Pink Hat

Ladies Group that is scheduled for this Saturday. I was explaining to her that this is very short notice for a cancellation." Lisa looked at Landry with her head bowed and her eyes looking up at her in question.

Mrs. Cartwright opened her mouth to say something but Landry interrupted her, "Oh, Mrs. Cartwright. I am so glad to meet you. I have heard wonderful things about you since I got here." Landy was putting it on thick and Mrs. Cartwright took the bait. "Oh…well…I,"

"Yes," Landry continued. "Everyone says that you are a strong woman who makes her own decisions and sticks to them. I can't remember just who told me but, someone even said that you could be the mayor yourself because you always take it upon yourself to go above and beyond in anything you are in charge of and put the wants and needs of the people of this town before your own personal feelings. High praise, indeed, Mrs. Cartwright. I must say that your reputation precedes you and I am very happy to finally meet you in person." Of course, this was all a lie. Landry had not even known that the mayor was married.

Mrs. Cartwright got a look of self pride on her face. She cleared her throat and addressed Lisa. "Lisa, my dear, I am afraid you misunderstood me. What I was trying to say is that we need to change the time on Saturday from 6pm to 7pm so that I won't have to cancel another engagement that I have that runs until 6:30. Of course, the caterers and set up committee will be here as usual to get everything set up."

Lisa smiled and replied, "Oh, Mrs. Cartwright. I am so

sorry for the mixup. Of course, the time change is perfectly fine. Absolutely fine. We will see you and your group then."

Mrs. Cartwright thanked them both and left with an extra pep in her step. Her self esteem seemed to have been boosted quite measurably. Lisa could barely wait until the door closed to ask Landry, "How in the world did you do that? She absolutely told me she wanted to cancel the event. She was adamant about it."

Landry smiled, "I ran into the mayor the other day and had a little run in with him. Seems he thinks it is uncouth for us to have a murder in our building. I straightened him out but I am sure he is the one who told his wife to cancel the event. I thought I would try to get her to use her own mind and not just automatically follow what her husband told her to do. Seems to have worked."

"Yes it did. I will say, you have more of your Aunt in you than I thought. Miss Tildie was very good at being kind and nice to people but getting her point across without them feeling threatened by her. I saw her come out in you just now."

Landry's eyes watered up. "That is the kindest thing you could have said to me, Lisa. Thank you." She abruptly went toward the elevator before she full on cried.

Chapter 10

Landry went into her apartment and freshened up a bit and made sure hair was still behaving itself and to replace the sneakers she was wearing with a pair of ankle boots. She ran by the kitchen to be sure that her new crock pot was working properly and it was. She went back out the door and through the lobby, where she told Lisa that she had an errand to run in her car and that she would be back later.

When she pulled up in her teal Bug in front of the bookstore, Ms. Millie was there waiting for her. She got in and said, "What is it with you and your aunt? What is the attraction to these tiny little vehicles? My knees will be screaming by the time we get back."

"Hello to you too, Ms. Millie. For me, a large vehicle makes me nervous. I feel like I am more in control in a smaller one. Plus, parking is much easier." Landry smiled.

It only took about 20 minutes to get to Fred's trailer with Ms. Millie giving explicit directions on how to get there. When they pulled up, there was an old, beat up blue pickup truck parked in front. Landry pulled up behind it. "Looks like someone is here. Let's just hope it is Melodie so I can ask her the questions I need to ask. Ms. Millie, you stay here. Lock the doors and I will go try to speak to Melodie. She might do better if we don't tag team her."

"I don't like it, Landry. This is a bad part of town and we don't know who all might be in that trailer. Maybe you should ask Wyatt or one of his deputies to come back with you just in case there is trouble." Ms. Millie looked worried.

"It will be fine. Besides, Wyatt would just tell me to leave it alone, but I was there when Melodie accused Portia of knowing something about Fred's death. He died in my building and I want to find out who did it as soon as possible. I sure don't want another threatening note slipped under my door, either. Just sit tight. If you see me running back, unlock the door so we can get out of here." Landry told her.

"Fine. But, I don't like it. Don't like it at all." Ms. Millie reiterated.

Landry got out of the car and heard the locks click behind her. She walked up to the raggedy porch and listened for a minute before she knocked. Not a sound. Not even anyone talking. She lightly tapped on the door. No answer, so she knocked harder. All of a sudden, the door to the trailer flew open and a tall, skinny, scary looking man with long blonde hair came charging out. He had a ball cap pulled low over his eyes. He knocked Landry to the floor of the porch and jumped over the railing. He landed on his feet and ran to the old truck parked in front of the Bug. He tore out of there so fast that the tires threw dirt and grass up on Landry's car.

When she got up off the floor, she looked out at the car. Ms. Millie was sitting there with her mouth hung open and her eyes as big as saucers. She was motioning to Landry to come on. Landry could make out her lips as Ms. Millie said, "Let's go."

Landry ignored her and turned toward the open trailer door. She stuck her head in and heard something or someone whining. She slowly made her way in, as she heard her car horn blasting outside. Ms. Millie was trying to get her to leave. The whining seemed to be coming from a back room. Landry yelled, "Is anyone there? Are you hurt?" No answer, just the whining. She went down the hallway and toward the sound. It appeared to be coming from a room that had the door closed. Landry gingerly opened the door. She stood there staring and shaking. "This cannot be happening to me." She said aloud. There, on the bed, lay the body of Melodie Leiton. Her throat was cut from one side to the other. Landry slowly bent down and felt for a pulse in the wrist that was thrown out to one side. Dead.

At that moment, Landry noticed that the whining was still going on. She looked around and saw a puppy. At least she thought it was a puppy. It could have been a very small older dog. It had brown and black markings and thick, puffy fur. Landry bent down to comfort it and the dog took off down the hall. Landry finally cornered it on the sofa and grabbed it up. She spoke comforting sounds to it as she hugged it and got the heck out of dodge.

She ran out of the trailer and managed to pull the door closed. She took the steps two at a time and ran to the car. She pulled on the door, but it was still locked so she yelled at Ms. Millie, "Open the door. We have to get outta here fast." Ms. Millie was looking straight ahead and shaking her head back and forth. "Nope. You are not putting that animal in the car with me." Landry looked at her like she had lost her mind. "Ms. Millie, it is just a puppy."

Ms. Millie was still shaking her head. She yelled through the window, "I do not like dogs. They are mean and have sharp teeth. Puppies have little sharp teeth and cut your skin wide open." Landry was flabbergasted. She thought for a minute and decided that Ms. Millie must have been bitten by a dog once. "Ok." Landry managed to put on her most determined face and looked Ms. Millie straight in the eyes. "Here is what is going to happen. You will unlock the doors. I will get in the back seat with this dog and not let it get anywhere near you. You will drive us to the Sheriff's Department. Got it?" Ms. Millie looked at her for a few seconds and said, "Only if you and that evil animal get on the passenger side of the back seat. I don't want that thing behind me where I can't see it."

"Fine." Landry walked around to the other side and Ms. Millie unlocked the door. Ms. Millie scooted over the gear shift into the driver's seat and then looked back at Landry and the dog. "Oh, Jesus." She shouted. "Why didn't you tell me you was hurt?" She then cranked the Bug up and took off so fast that Landry's head hit the back of the seat. She almost lost control of the dog, but managed to hold on. "Hurt? What are you talking about? Slow down, Ms. Millie."

About that time, Landry looked down to check on the dog. That's when she saw it. Her white shirt was covered in blood. Lots of blood. She looked at the dog and realized that he, too, was covered in blood. He must have been near enough to Melodie to get blood on him since he didn't appear to be injured. Landry looked up to tell Ms. Millie that she was not hurt and saw that they were swerving back and forth on the road. Landry thought to herself, "I didn't even think to ask Ms. Millie if she knew how to drive."

Landry started to speak up when she noticed that Ms. Millie's eyes were completely closed and she was praying, all the while going way too fast and from one lane to the other. "Lord, Jesus," Ms. Millie was saying, "please don't let this child die on my watch. Keep her in your loving arms, Lord, until I can get her to the hospital." Right about then, Landry noticed that they were headed for a ditch. She screamed, "I am not hurt. The dog got blood on me. Slow down or you will kill us all!"

That got Ms. Millie's attention and she opened her eyes just in time to slam on the brakes right before they hit the ditch. Landry's forehead hit the front seat and she lost control of the dog. It jumped into the front and Ms. Millie started screaming like she was being attacked by a pit bull. That scared the little dog and he jumped back to Landry and was shivering and even more frightened than Ms. Millie.

Landry sighed. "Ms. Millie, do you know how to drive a car?"

"Of course I do. I was driving before you were born."

"Well, then. Start driving…very slow this time, keep your eyes open and go straight to the Sheriff's Department. Melodie was in the trailer. She was dead and I think that man that jumped over me on the porch killed her."

Chapter 11

Ms. Millie did not say a word until they were in front of Wyatt in his office at the Sheriff's Department. When she did speak, she said, "I want to put on the official record right now that I did not think this was a good idea. Tell him, Landry. Tell him I tried to talk you out of it. Go ahead. Tell him."

Landry rolled her eyes and said, "Yes, Ms. Millie. You have stated that about five times since we walked into this building. I think Wyatt and everyone else knows that this was my idea and you did not approve of it."

Wyatt sat there and just stared at them. Ms. Millie was wild eyed, Landry was covered with blood and shaking and she was holding a dog. He was almost scared to ask what this idea had been, but he did.

"Well, she said that she wanted to go…" Ms. Millie started. Landry put up a hand to stop her. "I will tell the story, Ms. Millie." Ms. Millie looked miffed, but deferred to Landry.

"I mentioned to you, Sheriff, that when Adam and I were at the Sky High the other night, Melodie came bursting in and accused Portia of having something to do with Fred's death. I thought that if I caught Melodie at Fred's trailer that she might explain to me what she meant by that. I asked Ms. Millie to ride with me out there since she knew where the trailer was."

Ms. Millie jumped in again, "Wyatt, I didn't do

nothing but drive the car. I have to use the ladies room real bad. Can I go now?" Wyatt looked confused at the change of subject but said, "Yes. Of course you can Ms. Millie, but please wait outside on the bench by my office in case I need to talk to you further." She got up, gave Landry an evil look, walked out and slammed the door.

"Continue." was all that he said to Landry.

"Well, when I went up to the trailer door and knocked, a skinny, blonde haired man with a ball cap on opened it and ran slap over me. Knocked me down to the ground and jumped the porch railing. Oh, I forgot to mention that when we got there we saw an old, beat up, blue pickup truck parked in front of the trailer. Anyway, he took off running, jumped in the truck and got out of there fast." Landry continued to tell him the entire story and then stopped. She noticed that Wyatt's mouth was hanging open.

"Why in the world didn't you tell me there was a body out there as soon as you came in?" He hit a button on his phone and instructed his deputies to head out to the trailer. "That was something I needed to know right away, Landry."

At that moment, there was a knock on the door. Wyatt yelled, "Come in."

Landry looked towards the door and there stood Adam.

"Please tell me you weren't involved in this, too." Wyatt said to him as he put his hands on each side of his head like he had a headache.

Adam looked completely confused and said, "Uh, no. In fact, I am not even sure what "this" is. Ms. Millie had the desk deputy call me and tell me that Landry was at the Sheriff's Department and might need a lawyer. I came right here, even though if she actually does need one, I will have to call a criminal attorney, which I am not." He looked questionably at Landry.

Wyatt and Landry filled him in on what went on. Adam looked at Landry and said, "Why on earth would you do something like that? You could have been hurt or killed, not to mention Ms. Millie was with you."

Landry gave him a side glance and said, "Fred was killed in my building; I got a threatening note under my door; my residents are scared and anxious that whoever did it will come back. I was hoping that Melodie could explain to me why she thought Portia was involved."

Wyatt spoke up. "I was going to call both of you in tomorrow to tell you what we have found out so far. Landry, you have to promise me that you won't take anything else that I might tell you about this case and try to solve it yourself. I think this case is bigger than what any of us could have imagined and I don't have enough deputies to follow you around while we are busy working this murder investigation."

Landry looked properly scolded and said, "I won't do anything on the spur of the moment like this again. I was scared to death out there."

Wyatt looked at her for a minute and said, "We brought Portia in and interviewed her. She swears that she had nothing to do with Fred's murder and has no idea who did. She did tell me that in addition to working at Sky High singing, she is a waitress at the juke joint on the outskirts of town, 'The Purple Cactus'. Who comes up with these names?! Anyway, I asked her for somebody that could alibi her for the time that Fred was killed. She gave me the name of her boyfriend, Carl Garrison…they call him Scat. I got a deputy talking to Scat right now. We'll see how that pans out."

He leaned back in his chair and said, "And, even though you obviously think we aren't as smart as you are, Landry, we did bring Melodie in for an interview, too, before we interviewed Portia. She still insisted that Portia knew who was involved in this. I asked her why she was so sure and she clammed up. She said that it was my job to figure that out. I decided to let her go and talk to her again after I talked to Portia. Guess that is impossible now that she went and got her throat slit."

Adam winced and looked at Landry. "What are you going to do with the dog?" She smiled at the dog and said, "Tomorrow, I am going to the Vet's office just to see if by chance he has a microchip in him to tell us who he belongs to, although I fear he was Fred's or Melodie's dog, which makes him an orphan. If that is the case, I will keep him. I volunteered with an animal shelter in Bent Branch and I had been wanting to get a dog when things settled down. Maybe a cat, too. I will see what the Vet knows, if anything at all, about him tomorrow. For now, I think he is like Ms. Millie and needs to potty." She got up and looked at Wyatt, "Are you done with my interview?"

Wyatt sighed and said, "Yes but, Landry, I mean it.

Stay out of this and let us do our job. I don't want you getting hurt. Miss Tildie would haunt me."

"Funny, you are the second person who has said that to me." she said thoughtfully.

"Because it is the truth." Wyatt half laughed. "Listen, you and Adam take the dog out front and go into the side courtyard by the building. Let the dog do his business there since it is fenced in and you won't have to chase him far if he decides to play and run afterwards."

Landry thanked him and got several kleenex out of the box on his desk. He looked confused again. Landry laughed and said, "Look, if he has to do more than wee wee, I will pick it up and put it in the trash. I don't need any more trouble with the law." They all chuckled and she, Adam and the dog left. Ms. Millie was nowhere to be found. The deputy at the desk said she told him she had to get home and get her evening chores done and then told him that he needed to lose some weight so that he could chase down criminals.

The dog only had to wee wee and when they got back on the sidewalk, Landry started towards her car. She looked at her watch and realized that it was almost 6 o'clock. She turned to Adam and said, "You are still coming for dinner, right? I have it in the crock pot and it should be about done."

"Yep, if you still feel up to company after the day you've had."

"Actually, I would love the company. I do have a favor to ask, though. Since I don't want to scare everybody at the grocery store with this bloody shirt, could you run in there before you head to the apartment and grab a few things for me?"

"Sure. What do you need?" Adam got his phone out to write down the items.

"Let's see…puppy food, some small treats, puppy pads since I have no idea if this little ball of fur is house trained, and a couple of small toys for him. Hopefully, they will keep him from chewing on my things. Please tell them to put it on my account. I gave them my info already. That's all, I think. After tomorrow's Vet trip, I will see if I am going to keep him or not. I am really hoping that I can. For everything he has been through this afternoon, he has been very well behaved. Of course, he could just be scared."

"I am sure he is not only scared, but confused too. I'll grab the things and come on over. See you in a bit." Adam walked away.

When Landry walked into Magnolia Place, she saw Lisa sitting at the front desk. "What are you doing here Lisa? It's way past time for you to have gone home."

"I decided to wait on you and let you know in person that I think we have a pretty big problem.," Lisa answered.

"Oh no." Landry groaned. "If you only knew the day that I have had. I will fill you in later but what problem are you talking about?"

It was at that moment that Lisa noticed the dog that Landry was holding. "Well, when you tell me about your day please tell me why you are holding a dog and why you are completely covered in blood. Are you hurt? Just tell me if you're hurt." Lisa looked worried.

"No, I am absolutely not hurt and I will tell you the rest later. Please just tell me the problem we have." Landry sighed heavily.

Lisa looked only a tiny bit less worried to find out that Landry was not hurt. "I went upstairs to make sure that the event room was all cleaned up and ready for tomorrow. As I was walking around I noticed a painting missing. It is one of the most expensive paintings that your Aunt had in that room. In fact it was one of her favorites and that's the reason that she splurged on it. It's gone Landry. I am in shock, but it really truly is gone. Who could have taken it? I mean I'm always sitting here and if I'm not then Garrett or Fred or somebody is in this Lobby. How could somebody just walk out of the building with a painting that large?"

Landry could not speak. Her mind was numb and she could not form words. Finally, she asked, "Have you called the sheriff's department, Lisa? Do we happen to have a receipt or a picture of the painting or anything that we can give them to try to find it and see who took it?"

Lisa replied, "I waited to tell you before I called anyone. Yes, I do have a picture of the painting in a file. Your aunt made sure that we had pictures of all of the paintings, their worth and receipts for them. She put copies in her safe deposit box at the bank as well, and, I believe that she also gave copies to Adam to keep in her file at his office. She did all that in case there was a fire or some other disaster that destroyed the painting. I am sure that she never even imagined that someone would steal a painting off of the wall in the event room."

"Please call Wyatt and let him know. Lisa, I will pay you overtime if you can stay here and show them to the Event Room and where the painting was located. I need to go up and wash blood off of me and the dog. Adam ran by the store to pick up a few things for the dog. He is supposed to come straight here when he is done shopping. We are supposed to have dinner tonight, which I have in the crock pot in my apartment, but it looks like it may be a midnight snack instead. As soon as he gets here and can stay with the dog I will go up to the fifth floor and talk to Wyatt."

"No problem," said Lisa. "I will stay as long as you need me. This has really shaken me up; I don't like the fact that someone came into this building and stole a painting right under my nose. I will call Wyatt right now and explain everything. Oh, and Landry, don't worry about explaining your clothes and the dog to me. I will get Adam to fill me in."

Landry thanked Lisa and went upstairs. She immediately went to the kitchen and turned the crockpot on warm, grabbed two large freezer bags and then went into the bathroom and ran a tub of water. She washed the dog with her shampoo and then towel dried him and let him run. She was so tired and still had a night ahead of her. She would worry about whatever the dog messed up later. After she had drained the tub, she heard a knock on the door. She ran into the living room and said, "Who's there?"

"That's my girl. You can't be too careful." She was so glad to hear Adam's voice. She let him in and told him that she had washed the dog but that she now had to wash herself and change before heading upstairs to the event room.

"Yeah," Adam sighed and shook his head. "Lisa told me. I hate that, Landry. Miss Tildie cherished her paintings. It makes me so angry that somebody took one of them. I wonder if it was the same person that killed Fred?"

"I had not even thought about that. I will ask Wyatt what he thinks. Right now, I am heading into the shower. Do you mind being on dog duty until I get back down here? Obviously, dinner will be extremely late tonight." she said as she was walking towards the bathroom.

"No problem on either count. I will watch the furball and dinner will be whenever you are calm enough to eat."

"Speaking of that, I just realized that I didn't have one anxiety attack during all of this mess today. Do you think my body is getting used to being in a constant state of worry? That would just be sad." Landry frowned.

"I am not a doctor, but maybe you are just learning to handle your anxiety better now that you are responsible for so many different things. I am happy that you didn't have a panic attack today, though. I worry about you when you have them." Adam said.

Landry turned towards the bathroom and smiled. It had been a long time since she had someone in her life that truly worried about her.

She removed her clothes and placed the bloody t-shirt and boots in separate freezer bags and zipped them up. She stayed in the hot shower longer than she normally would have. She washed and washed, even though she had no blood directly on her skin. She scrubbed until she finally felt clean. She put on a clean t-shirt, some sweatpants, socks and another pair of boots. Then she grabbed her wet hair and put it in a bun on the back of her neck. She knew that as soon as it started to dry, her hair would frizz up and look atrocious, but she didn't have time to dry it. She grabbed the freezer bags and headed to the den, where Adam and the dog were.

"Ok. I am going upstairs to meet with Wyatt. It should not take long at all and I will be back so we can eat. Thanks for staying with the dog. He looks right at home, doesn't he?" She laughed. The dog had curled up on a couch pillow and had his little toy beside him. He was fast asleep. She told Adam bye and went upstairs.

There wasn't much to do when she got there. Lisa had sent her a message saying she was heading home. Wyatt was the only one in the event room since he said his deputies were out at the Purple Cactus speaking with the owner about Portia as a follow up. He noticed that Landry was carrying something. "What is that in your hands?" he asked her.

"Oh." She looked down at the freezer bags she was holding. "I put my bloody shirt and shoes in these bags. I thought you might want them for evidence or something."

Wyatt looked surprised. "This is great, Landry. I should have mentioned that to you. After you told me about Melodie being dead, all I could think of was to get someone out to that trailer ASAP. Thanks for getting these to me."

He took the items from Landry.

"Well, like almost every person I know, I do watch crime shows, read crime books and watch the news. I guess I have heard about law enforcement needing all the evidence in a case and I remembered that when I was taking these things off to get a shower." Landry smiled at him.

"I wanted to let you know that I got a call as soon as you and Adam left the office. Seems one of our wealthy full time residents had a break in. Guess what was stolen?"

Landry thought for a second and her eyes got big, "A painting?"

"Yep. A very expensive painting. I got a deputy up there now getting the details. I have also told the owner of our local Art Gallery, Sylvia Weathers, to make sure all of her security features are in place and monitored. I want to have all bases covered."

Landry nodded. "Do you think that these thefts are associated with the deaths of Fred and Melodie? Also, since the victims are brother and sister, I wonder if there is a familial connection to the deaths."

Wyatt spoke up, "We have looked at that angle, too. The problem with the family connection is that Fred and Melodie are the only members left in their immediate family and both of their parents were only children. Marge said they are having a time at the coroner's office. There are no next of kin contacts to be found. She said we might have to have a pauper's funeral for the siblings unless someone comes forward. But, I definitely think the same person is stealing the paintings."

"That is so very sad. I mean, I am an only child but I do have cousins and family on my father's side. Just seems unreal that the Leiton's have nobody." Landry looked down at the floor.

"Lisa has already shown me where the painting was hanging in this room and she also gave me the copies of it and information from the files she keeps. We will put it out there in the media and contact any known black market art places that we are aware of in case the person tries to sell it. I do have to tell you that the painting may be already in another country by now. It is very hard to get these things back, depending on how smart the thief is. I am sure Miss Tildie had insurance on all of them so at least you can recoup your loss. I also know how much these paintings meant to her and my goal is to get it back intact."

"Thanks, Wyatt. I appreciate you coming over here to pick up the information. I know you will do all that you can to get it back. Is there anything else we need to discuss?"

"Nope, that's it for now. I need to get back to the office and see what my deputies have found out about Portia, as well as the theft up on the mountain. Have a good night, Landry." They walked out and Landry locked the door back.

When she returned to the apartment, she went into the den. Adam was watching the news on television and the dog was curled up next to him. Adam told her that he put a puppy pad down in the den and that the dog had actually used it. He said he also put one next to the balcony door in the living room. He had bought some doggie bowls when he was at the store and had put water and food down on a towel in the corner of the kitchen. He seemed to have it all under control.

Landry told him what Wyatt had said about the other theft of a painting and also caught him up on what was going on with the murder investigation. When she was done informing him of what she had learned, she went to the bathroom to wash up. She then went to the kitchen and set the table. She dished both of them up some of the chicken, dressing and green beans from the crockpot, added a heaping spoon of the cranberry sauce on the side and put a slice of the bread on both plates. She grabbed two glasses and made them both some sweet tea. By the time she was done making the plates, Adam had gotten to the kitchen, after washing up in the bathroom.

"It smells so good in here, Landry. My stomach was growling waiting for you to get back. Thanks for doing this for us. You have had such a long, hard day." Adam was practically licking his lips in anticipation of the food.

"It's a good thing that I decided to throw this in the crock pot earlier today or we would have had to get takeout. I've a feeling that after eating this warm meal, I will sleep very well tonight." Landry laughed. "I sure will be glad to go to the Vet's office tomorrow. I hope he has some information on the dog and what his name is. I hate just calling him dog or puppy."

They finished their meal and put the dishes in the dishwasher. As they were doing this, Adam said, "You know, that meal was kind of like Thanksgiving in a Crock Pot." He laughed.

Landry replied, "Yes it is. I never thought of that." As she was putting the leftovers in the fridge, she saw the strawberries. "Oh no. I forgot all about dessert. Would you like some now?" She tried to cover up a yawn.

"I don't think so. You need to get some sleep and I am full as a tick. Maybe we can have it another time." Adam closed the door on the dishwasher. "I need to get going anyway. I have an early meeting in the morning."

Landry walked him to the door and the dog joined them. "I think we may have really bonded." Adam said as he bent down to pet the dog on the head. "I sure hope you both sleep well tonight. Please let me know what you find out tomorrow at the Vet's office."

Landry assured him that she would and locked the door behind him. She turned out the lights in the apartment and went to the bedroom to put on her nightclothes. When she was done with that, she noticed that the dog was not there with her. She went into the den and saw that he had used his puppy pad. He seemed to be good at picking up things pretty fast. She added a puppy pad to her bedroom and put him on the bed with her. She snuggled him for a few minutes and then he laid down on the bottom of the bed and went to sleep. It took Landry longer to fall asleep. She just kept thinking about the murders, the theft and who could have done it.

Chapter 12

When she awoke the next morning, the dog was still on the bed with her. She did notice, however, that his puppy pad was wet which meant that he must have gotten down from the bed to use the pad and then got back up in the bed. Landry wondered how such a little doggie could jump that high but was glad that he was able to do it and not wake her up. It wasn't long that she found the answer to her question. She had a reading chair beside her bed and the puppy jumped on it and then jumped on the bed to roll around and grunt. He looked so happy.

She went to the kitchen and put down dog food and water and also turned on the coffee pot. She would be taking coffee to go this morning, so she needed to make more than one cup. She went into the bathroom to shower and dress. When she was done and went back to the kitchen, the dog was sitting there like he knew they were going somewhere. She filled a cup with coffee, grabbed a banana and went out on the balcony; the dog followed her. The balcony wall was solid with no slats so there was no worry of him falling through. They sat there until she finished her coffee and banana and then went back in for her to fill up an insulated cup to take with her. About that time, Landry's phone rang. She looked at the number and grinned. "What's up, buttercup?" she said as she answered. It was her best friend in the entire world, Annie, from Bent Branch. Landry pictured her like she looked the day Landry left to come here. Annie was standing there telling Landry goodbye and she was hiccuping from crying so much. Her black mascara was running all down her face and her hot pink hair that was cut in a short pixie cut was blowing in the wind. Landry got misty eyed thinking about it.

Annie was talking in her usual fast way. "Girrrl…I miss you so much. It is hectic at the bakery as usual. Two of my helpers quit on the same day for different reasons and I am training new ones." Annie owned the only bakery in Bent Branch and did a huge amount of business. Everyone loved her pastries, donuts, cakes and all the rest. "Also, Blaine and I broke up."

"What? I thought the two of you were on the path to marriage. What in the world happened?"

"Well, I thought that, too.," Annie said. "But, it seems that Blaine was on another song page. He came for dinner one night and left his cell on my couch. I picked it up to put a sweet note on it before I returned it and, well you know how nosy I am. I pulled up his sent messages and, Landry, I almost blew a gasket. He has been seeing another woman. A woman here in town that I despise. They were making plans to go outta town the following week when he knew I would be swamped at the bakery and wouldn't be able to breathe, much less worry about where he was. I had two weddings and three birthdays that I had to do cakes and other things for. Anyway, I confronted him and he didn't even deny it. I called him things I didn't even know that my brain knew about. It's over."

"Oh, Annie, I am so sorry. I am glad that you found

out this about him now before you got married to the jerk, though."

"So am I. How are things going in Bobwhite Mountain? Are you bored to tears and want to come back here to your best friend and the library yet?" Annie asked hopefully.

Landry chuckled that she was not ready to do that and they talked for a long time while she filled her friend in on everything that had happened so far. Annie gasped and said, "Wow...you haven't let the grass grow under your feet. I am going to have to visit when I get my head above water here. Sounds like an interesting place." They hung up and Landry thought about their friendship. They didn't speak everyday, but Annie was the sister she had never had. She sure would be glad when she could see her again. She grabbed her coffee and the puppy and they left the apartment.

When they got to the lobby, she spoke to Garrett and then asked Lisa for directions to the Vet's office in town. She nodded when she realized that his office was very near Mr. Harcourt's. About that time, the elevator opened and Landry recognized Logan and Everly Watson from the meet and greet. They had their twins with them. She greeted them, "Hi, Mr. and Mrs. Watson. Good to see you again."

Everyly spoke up, "Please call us Logan and Ev. These are our twins, Bridget and Ridge. Logan took the day off today so that he could go with us to their 2 year checkup." Ev pointed to the double stroller.

Landry squatted down and told the adorable twins hello. When she stood up, Logan asked her, "Miss Burke, has there been any progress on the murder that took place in the building. I worry about Ev being at home with the twins when I am at work."

Landry stood back up and answered, "First off, please call me Landry. And, they are making some progress on the case. From what I understand it is very complicated but the Sheriff's Department is spending the majority of their time…as well as overtime…on this case. Just so you know, I am also working with someone to get security cameras installed in the building. I think that will help all of us to feel more secure." She knew from the meet and greet that Logan was doing his residency at the hospital to be a Pediatrician and that Ev was a stay at home mom to their twins.

About that time the dog, who Lisa had been holding, jumped down and ran up to the stroller and whined. The twins laughed and Landry explained that she had found the dog and wasn't sure yet if she would be keeping it. The twins petted it a few more times and then the Watson family headed for the garage.

"I heard you mention the security cameras." Lisa said. "Mr. Mayhew dropped a file off for you. It is a cost estimate for installing the cameras on each floor, the lobby and the garage. He said you could let him know if you wanted his company to proceed."

"Thanks, Lisa. I will get it to Mr. Harcourt and get him to approve the expense. Since we had a murder in the building, I don't think he will have any other choice than to give the ok. Also, Lisa, I need to find a new doctor here in town. Who would you recommend I see?"

Lisa didn't even have to think about it. "Dr. Freeman. She is wonderful and is my doctor. I will write her number down if you like or I can just text it to you. She is in the new healthcare building by the hospital."

"Please just text it to me. I need to show her my meds and get a checkup. It is time, anyway, and since I have moved here now I need to get established with someone. I am heading to the Vet's Office…what did you say his name was?" Lisa replied, "Dr. Portman."

"Got it. I will check in with you later." Landry picked up the dog and went to the parking garage. She decided to drive to the Vet's office since she had other things to do that day that would require a car.

When she got to the Vet's office, she filled out the required paperwork and sat down with the dog in lap. It was only a few minutes until they called them back and put them in a room. A few seconds later, the door opened. "Hello, I am Dr. Portman. Very nice to meet you Miss Burke."

"Please, call me Landry."

"Alright, Landry, and who is your little friend?"

"Well, that is what I am hoping you can tell me. See, I found him and I was wondering if you recognized him from a visit his former owner may have brought him here for."

Dr. Portman picked up the dog and immediately said, "I do, actually. This is Fred Leiton's dog that he got about 8 months ago. He said a friend of his had a new litter of puppies and Fred fell for this one and adopted him. Fred brought him here for his first shots and to make sure the dog was healthy."

"I was afraid of that. I found him at Fred's trailer. You see, Dr. Portman, I own the building that Fred was murdered in. I mean, he was my employee. I inherited the apartment building and bookstore from my Aunt Tildie."

"Ah, yes. Your aunt was one of our benefactors at the animal shelter I set up. I pretty much fund it on my own right now with donations given to us by the citizens of the town. When my wife, Tara, finishes nursing school, we will be able to put more money in it and help even more animals. Your Aunt was a very kind person and we all miss her terribly. Horrible thing about Fred. I was shocked when I heard. I thought his sister, Melodie, would take the dog since she stayed with Fred when she was in town."

"Well, she may have intended to do just that, but unfortunately she met her untimely demise, too. Please don't spread that around since I am not sure how many people are aware of it yet." Landry pleaded.

"Don't worry. Being a doctor, I am excellent at holding confidences. Let's just check out Pep, here, and make sure he is alright."

"Pep?" Landry asked.

"That's what Fred named the puppy. Said he had a dog from his childhood that was named Pepper that he loved to pieces. Fred shortened the name and named this little guy, Pep."

"I really don't care for that name. Do you think Pep would adjust to a new name?" Landry asked him.

"Sure. He is only 8 months old. I would give you a suggestion, though. Think about giving a name that sounds close to 'Pep'. That will make it easier for him to respond to it right away. Now, he seems to be just fine. In case you are interested in his background, Pep is a YorkiePom. Seems his original owners had a Yorkie and a friend of theirs had a pomeranian. They went out to eat one night and locked the Yorkie in a bedroom and left the Pomeranian in the den since the Pom was in heat. When they got back, the bedroom door was open and both dogs were asleep on the bed. Pep here was an 'oopsie' puppy, along with his 4 brothers and sisters." Dr. Portman laughed. "He will only get to be around 8 pounds. You got yourself a tiny dog, Landry."

"I guess I do. Which works out well since I live in my apartment building on an upper floor." She smiled.

"He should be fine using one of those puppy pads for his business. These little guys don't put out much, if you get my drift."

"I do and he has already proven that he uses those pads well." She laughed. "Thank you, Dr. Portman. I am so relieved that Fred took good care of the dog. I will also make an appointment to come back and have him microchipped just in case he makes a break for it."

"Sounds great. Please call me Eric, Landry. We are both property owners in the community and should be on a first name basis. Also, my wife will be glad to give you any tips on things in town if you need it. Just give her a call at the daycare out on Church Street where she works part time. Like I mentioned, she is going to school to be a nurse but she took a year off to spend time with our son, Kane. He is a year old now and she says she is waiting until he turns two to start back to school. We will see if she actually does it." He smiled.

"Thank you so much, Eric. Also, I volunteered at the animal shelter in my hometown. I will be doing that here, if that's alright, and I will also be making a donation. It is wonderful that you have taken on the shelter even though you are so busy with work." Landry told him goodbye as he thanked her for her generosity.

As she got back in the car after leaving Dr. Portman's office, she got a message on her phone from Wyatt for her to call him. She did and he said, "Hey, Landry. Thanks for calling me. My deputies found Carl Garrison, otherwise known as Scat. He has agreed to come in for questioning and the deputies are following him back to the department. I was wondering if you could drop by here and look through our one way window outside the interrogation room and see if he was the one you saw leaving Fred's trailer. The deputies said he was driving a beat up old blue pickup with no tailgate. I called Ms. Millie to see if she would come but she informed me that as soon as she saw the door of the trailer fly open, she ducked down so that whoever it was wouldn't see her and kill her. She says that when she looked back up, you were getting up off the porch and the truck was flying out of the yard."

"Sure, Wyatt. I am going to run the dog back to my apartment first. Seems the little fellow did belong to Fred, so I am adopting him. Let me message Lisa and she can grab him from my car and take him up to my apartment. I won't be long."

"Sounds good. Do me a favor though. When you get here, park your car behind the Department in the employee lot and I will text you when we get Scat inside and in a room. Just to be safe, I don't want him to recognize you or the Bug."

Landry drove to Magnolia Place and Lisa got Pep out of the car to take him to the apartment.

Next, she did exactly what Wyatt asked and waited until he texted her that it was ok to come on in. When she was outside the interrogation room, she stared at the man sitting at the table and sighed.

"That's not who I saw, Wyatt. This guy has black hair and is tall and bulky. The guy at the trailer was also tall, but he was very slim and had longer, blonde hair. Even just seeing him from the back as he was running, I know this is not him."

"Alright. We are getting his DNA anyway and we got Portia's too. So far, he is swearing that he has no idea who killed Fred or Melodie. He has a record for petty theft and not paying child support. Nothing criminal, though."

"Sorry, Wyatt. This case seems like it gets more confusing all the time. I wish I could have been of some help. I do wonder about the truck, though. It sounds like the same one that left the trailer before I found Melodie. When

I leave, I am going to drive by out front and see if it is the same one. I will text you afterwards to let you know."

Wyatt walked back in the interrogation room and Landry went to her car. She drove by the front parking lot and saw the truck. There was no mistaking it. She drove two streets over to a place called "The Takeout King" that everyone had told her had the best fries in town. She pulled into a parking spot and sent Wyatt a text. "Same truck. No doubt about it." Then, she sent Adam a text and told him about the Vet's appointment. She ended it with, "So, looks like I am the proud owner of an 8 month old Yorkie/Pom. Name to be decided at a later date." Adam texted her back right away with "Yay" and a smiley face.

She pulled in the drive thru and ordered a large fry and a diet coke. When she got to the window to pay she held out her hand with the money in it. She heard a loud crash and turned her head to see what was going on. The drive thru attendant heard it too, and instead of taking Landry's money, she wasn't paying attention and punched her arm out the window and right into the side of Landry's head. The attendant's ring cut the side of Landry's face. "Ouch." Landry screamed. The attendant turned around and looked mortified. She grabbed napkins from the counter and shoved them at Landry. "Oh no…I am so, so sorry."

The attendant apologized several more times and refused to take Landry's money. "It's on the house. Please come back to see us. My Dad is going to be furious about this. He owns this place and lets me work here to make some extra dough." Landry looked at the girl's horrified face and noticed her nametag. "Look, Kylie, he will never know. It was an accident and don't worry, I will be back." She mustered a smile. She never did see what all the commotion was about with the crash.

After eating her fries and drinking her diet coke (the coffee from this morning was long gone), she drove to Mr. Harcourt's office to drop off the estimate for the security cameras. She was glad to find that he was out of the office and she left the file along with a note for him with his receptionist.

She got back to the garage and entered Magnolia Place. Lisa was sitting with her head in her hands and Garrett looked like he had lost his best friend. "What is wrong?" Landry asked.

"It's Mr. Larson, one of our residents on the second floor. He had a wreck a little while ago. They just called us from the hospital wanting his son's phone number. Mr. Larson ran a red light and hit a truck. He is in ICU in critical condition." Lisa was crying. "He is just such a kind man. He ran the Feed and Seed here in town before he retired. When his wife passed away, he sold his house and moved here so that he could be around people and socialize. I pray that he will be alright, Landry."

"I remember meeting him. James Larson, right? He was joking and seemed so happy to be living here. Where does his son live? Is he coming here?"

"Yes. He lives in Michigan. He called me after the hospital called him. He is getting a flight out today. He is the only family Mr. Larson has since Mrs. Larson passed away. His son is married with two little boys."

A thought hit Landry at that moment. "Lisa, I think I heard that wreck. I was in the drive thru at The Takeout King and heard a loud crash. I never saw what happened but I am sure that was Mr. Larson's accident I heard."

Garrett spoke up, "Yes, Miss Burke. It had to be. The intersection that the hospital said Mr. Larson ran the light on is on the same street as The Takeout King. In fact, he was probably going there to pick up food. He loves that place." Garrett shook his head. "Horrible thing, horrible thing."

"Please let me know if we hear anymore about him. I know they won't let us see him but, after his son gets here, I will go visit. I will pray for Mr. Larson and also add him to our church prayer list."

Garrett spoke up, "Miss Burke, what happened to the side of your face? It seems it is bleeding a little."

Landry said, "Oh, just a little mishap. Nothing to worry about. Actually, Garrett, you probably should get used to it. I am an accident just waiting to happen."

She walked to the elevators and went to her apartment. She heard whining behind the door and knew that the puppy was waiting for her. She didn't want him to disturb the others on the floor, so she decided that she would leave him in the den in the back of the apartment from now on. She would put all of his things in there and leave the tv on low for him and the drapes open to let in some light. Maybe he at least wouldn't whine so much then. She went in and picked him up. "Hey, sweet puppy. Have you had a good day so far?" He licked her face and buried his head in her shoulder. She decided she had to get him a collar and leash so she could take him for walks. She put him back on the floor and checked his puppy pads. He had used them and she also noticed that he had eaten his food and drank his water. It seemed like he was getting used to her and his new home. She went to the bathroom and put some antibiotic cream on the tiny cut on her face and then covered it with a small band aid.

She called down to speak to Lisa. When she answered, Landry asked her, "Do Lenny and Carl also do the maintenance at the bookstore?"

"Yes they do. Miss Tildie put that in their contracts. Is something wrong over there?"

"No. I was wondering if you could ask them to run over there when they have a minute and move the things from the small storage room at the back of the bookstore and put them in the larger storage room. We are going to make that smaller room a Children's Room. I also need to find someone to paint and lay carpet in there for me. Any ideas?"

Lisa said, "Sure, I will get them to move the things tomorrow. As far as the painting goes, they can do that, too, no problem. I will have to contact someone in town to lay the carpet. We have a couple of flooring places close that can probably do that for you. I will check with them and then you can run by one day and pick out what you want or even go online and pick it out there. What color do you want the walls? We have an account at the local hardware store so that the guys can pick up the paint and supplies they need."

"Just white is fine. I may find someone to do a couple of murals for me."

"That sounds lovely, Landry. The kids will be so excited. Hey, I just thought of something. When you get a chance, run by the art gallery. I bet Sylvia knows someone to do the murals. She knows all the artists in town. She owns the gallery." Lisa suggested.

"That is a wonderful idea, Lisa. I will drop by there one day. I have been meaning to visit anyway to look around. Thanks for the tip."

"No problem. Uh-oh, I see Cecil across the street at the bookstore and I don't have all of the mail ready for him to take. Let me go, Landry. He gets so testy if everything isn't ready when he gets here." Lisa hung up and Landry laughed. Cecil sure did have everybody on their toes when it came to the mail.

Chapter 13

Landry was getting ready to do some cleaning in her apartment when her phone rang. She answered and it was Wyatt. "Landry, I have a couple of updates for you. We finally got the DNA results from the bathroom on the fifth floor. Unfortunately, there is no matching DNA in CODIS, the program where all the DNA is entered into for cross checking. It also did not match Portia or Scat. It did, however, tell us that whoever killed Fred is a female. We are still waiting on results from Melodie's crime scene in the trailer. This case is getting curiouser and curiouser. I really thought Scat was going to be our perp."

"That is frustrating. I am guessing that the DNA from Fred's crime scene didn't belong to Melodie?" Landry asked.

"Nope. Believe me, her DNA is in CODIS. She had several run-ins with the law in her time on this earth. What is very interesting is that Portia has connections to everybody in both the thefts and the murders. You remember I told you about the couple up on the mountain that also had a painting stolen? It was Brad and Lucy Pugh."

"The owners of the Sky High where Portia works part time singing?"

"Yep. We are getting on the right track, I can feel it in my bones. Just seems like we hit a dead end everywhere we turn. Also, we checked and the only DNA on the note you got was yours. Whoever wrote it and put it under your door must have been wearing gloves. Anyway, I just thought I would fill you in. Gotta run now. I have a meeting with our mayor that I am not looking forward to. He seems to think the murders were concocted by his opposition to make him look bad. What a joke he is." Wyatt hung up.

Landry looked down at Pep and said, "I have to figure out a new name for you, don't I? First we have to do some cleaning up. Let's listen to some music. I think I am in the mood for some old rock music."

She pulled up her music app on her phone and started scrolling through her saved music. Music always calmed her nerves and helped her to think better. She looked at Pep and said "I think it is a Zep kind of day. Upon hearing that, Pep ran up to her and yipped. She looked down at him, "You like Zeppel..." Before she finished the sentence, Pep yipped two more times and tried to climb up her leg. "What in the world? Then it hit her. "YES. Pep and Zep sound just alike. Your new name is Zep." At that, Zep started twirling in circles and yipped again. Landry laughed. "I agree. It's perfect. You think it is your old name and I love their music."

After she had cleaned up, Landry made her a bagel with cream cheese and olives and a fresh cup of coffee. She had already fed Zep so they both went out on the balcony to sit down. As she ate her bagel she thought to herself that she really needed to start cooking meals more often so that she would have leftovers and not eat snacky things all the time. She had just finished her bagel when her phone rang.

It was Adam. "Whew. I have had a busy day. I just got a chance to breathe. I wanted to ask you if you would like to go out to the farm Sunday after church. My sister, Ivy, is flying in from San Diego since her nursing job there is done. She heads to Florida next but is spending a week with Mom before she has to report there. Aunt Denise and Uncle Steve have invited us to have lunch with them at the farm. I think Lisa will be there, too."

"I would love to. It will be so good to be there again and I can't wait to meet Lisa's parents and your sister. Will we leave straight from church?"

"Yes. As a matter of fact, I am picking Mom and Ivy up before church and then we will swing by for you. That way, we can all ride together. I know I will see you before Sunday but I just wanted to ask you before you made other plans." Adam explained.

"Those plans sound perfect. Adam, I was thinking. Wyatt is working awfully hard on these thefts and murders. I saw him today and he looked bone tired. Wonder if we could arrange for you and him to come over tomorrow night for dinner here at my apartment? I just told myself that I needed to cook and eat real food and not just takeout or snacks and I hate cooking a big meal for just myself. Tomorrow is Friday so maybe Wyatt will have time to at least come by and eat a good meal."

"That sounds great to me. I was going to ask you to go eat somewhere tomorrow night anyway but, this way I can spend some time with the puppy, too."

"You two have really bonded. Also, if you can, come

by tonight for dessert and coffee. I have some updates on the case to tell you that Wyatt passed along to me today."

"Will do. I just saw that I had a missed call from Wyatt. I will just wait and hear it all from you. I am going to order a sandwich and eat that while I am doing all this paperwork from today's meetings. As soon as I am done with that, I will text you and let you know I am on the way. Bye."

"Bye." Landry replied. She looked at the clock and it was 3pm. She decided to finish cleaning up and then go to the hardware store to get Zep a collar and leash as well as another food and water bowl to put on the balcony. She would come back and give him a walk before they settled in for the night.

She got to the lobby and didn't see Lisa or Garrett. Then, she noticed that Fred's replacement, Josh, was at the lobby assistants' desk. "Hi, Josh. I forgot you came in at noon. Garrett now works from 4am till noon, right?" She asked him.

"Yes, ma'am, and the other new guy, Zack, comes in at 8pm to relieve me and stays until Garrett is back at 4am. I thought I was just going to be part time but Lisa said the other guys agreed for us all to have 8 hour shifts with an hour long lunch break." He was almost, but not quite, as formal as Garrett.

About that time, Lisa walked up. "Hi, Landry. How is everything going with the puppy?" Landry explained to her everything she learned at the Vet's office and also about Zep's new name.

"I was talking to Josh just now and thought of something. I know all the doormen, or lobby assistants as I would prefer them to be called, work 8 hour shifts all week. What do we do on the weekends? I mean, they can't work 7 days a week." Landry exclaimed.

"Well, that is something I was going to talk to you about. As you know, Miss Tildie didn't have weekend coverage in the lobby. When you told me that you preferred to have 24/7 coverage, I knew we would have to hire someone else but, with Fred's death I thought we should hire his replacement and a third doorma…uh, lobby assistant, before I brought the weekend coverage up. I can't believe you haven't noticed that nobody is here on the weekends before now." Lisa smiled.

"I guess between trying to get settled in, making sure the bookstore is running ok, the thefts, the murders, the dog…I just wasn't paying attention. Sorry, Lisa. I know I have put a lot on you since I have been here." Landry apologized.

"No, no. I love what I do and I can do it in a third of the time that you can since I have been here so long. Anyway, do you remember Orvis Nelson from the meet and greet? He lives on the 3rd floor." She asked Landry.

"I do. I thought that he had a very "old timey" name for a man as young as he is. Not that there's anything wrong with that…I love names from the past. Very unique and easy to remember." She smiled and Lisa continued.

"Well, Orvis works at a car dealership in the next town over, Wrigley Springs. He only works weekdays and doesn't make a lot of money. He asked me if we ever had something come up where he could work weekends here or at the bookstore to please let him know. I was thinking that maybe we could get him to work 9am till 9pm on Saturday and Sunday. I know that would still leave some time without coverage but, when you get the security cameras maybe we can connect those to your phone so that you can check the lobby every now and then just to be sure everything is ok. Of course, Orvis would lock the front door when he went up for the night and the residents would have to use their key cards to get in the lobby, which most of them do at night anyway."

"I know Mr. Harcourt is going to balk at that. He already said we don't need 3 lobby assistants. I explained to him that they do so much more than just man the door. Speaking of, where is Josh?" Landry noticed he wasn't at the desk.

"He is doing some of those things you are talking about. He goes up on the floors before I leave to be sure everything is in order and to dust the tables and benches in the hallways. He also cleans the outdoor grill area and empties the trash out there, as well as all of the other trash cans inside. Then, he locks the elevators down here in the lobby and cleans and vacuums them and then vacuums the lobby. I printed out flyers and gave them to all the residents to let them know that the elevators would be out of commission for about 20 minutes everyday between 3 and 4, in case they push the button and no elevator comes to the floors. They were all fine with it. He does all of this before

I leave so that I am here to greet anyone that may come in. When he is done with that, he sweeps the garage area and makes sure the carts are placed correctly in the corral."

Landry looked confused. "I thought you told me that we had local maids come in several times a week to do those kinds of things."

Lisa smiled, "Not anymore. I figured that if we were getting all this extra help, they should earn their pay. When Zack comes in, I have left him duties that he can do while sitting at the desk. Since he is a computer programmer, I knew he would have to be good at computer work. I leave instructions about flyers that I need printed, letters that need typing, rent notices, and other things that I can get off of my plate. He also does the flyers and posters for the bookstore, since that took up a lot of my time. With the money you are saving on housekeeping coming in, you can pay Orvis to work on weekends and still have some leftover. Orvis has agreed to do the light housekeeping on the weekends, too. I told the housekeeping service that we may need them on certain occasions, but not full time anymore. They understood and said to just give them a call if and when we needed their service."

"Lisa, I think that with the extra money I have in the budget after paying Orvis to work weekends, I am giving you a raise. You run this place and I absolutely know that it would go to seed if you weren't here." Landry reached over and gave her a hug. "Now, what I really needed to know was where the hardware store is located. I need to get a collar and leash for Zep and also a couple of other things."

Lisa told her, "You know when you were at the Takeout King earlier today? Just keep going down that road and it is on the right hand side. Barry's Hardware. You can't miss it. He has a huge wrench out front for his sign." Lisa cackled when she said that.

Landry thanked her and went to the garage just as Josh began to vacuum the elevators. She found the hardware store with no problem. That huge wrench out front with "Barry's Hardware" written on it was as easy to find as Lisa had said. She got the collar, leash, two more bowls and some extra treats for Zep and headed home. When she got back to the apartment, Zep wasn't whining at the door. Landry almost had a panic attack when she walked in and he wasn't there to greet her. She started twisting her ring and ran to the bedroom. He wasn't there. Then, she remembered that she left the tv on in the den. She walked in there and saw Zep laying on the sofa with his head on a couch pillow and one of his toys under his paw. The tv was on the Animal Planet channel on low volume. She walked over and flipped the tv off. When she turned around, Zep had popped his head up and started bouncing on the couch, wanting her to pick him up. She did and put his collar and leash on. He wasn't quite comfortable with that yet but, when she said "let's go for a walk, Zep." he started running to the front door.

They took a walk to the park and stayed for about half an hour before she got a text from Adam. He was on his way to her apartment. She and Zep walked back and got there before Adam did. She took off Zep's leash and he went flying to the kitchen to make sure his bowls were still there. Landry laughed but was glad that he was feeling at home here. She looked at the clock. It was 6pm. She went to the kitchen and put on a pot of coffee and got the strawberries out to wash. In just a few minutes, she heard a knock on the door. She let Adam in and Zep came flying in the room, yipping and dancing all around. Adam petted him and when Zep calmed down, Landry told Adam to come sit in the kitchen so that she could fill him in on things while she prepared their dessert. She told him everything that she had learned from Wyatt; told him about Zep's new name and how he got it; told him what a phenomenal manager his cousin, Lisa, was and about her and Zep's visit to the park. She took out the pound cake and two bowls. She put a big slice in each bowl and loaded on the strawberries. While she was whipping the heavy cream, Adam poured them each a cup of coffee. She put the whipped cream on top of the strawberries and they carried it all to the balcony. They sat at Landry's little round table out there and enjoyed their dessert and coffee while Zep walked around and discovered that he now had water and food bowls out there, too.

"That was amazing, Landry. Just what I needed after today. By the way, I talked to Wyatt for a split second today. We were beside each other at a stop light in town. He said he would love to come over tomorrow night for dinner. He looked like I had offered him a million bucks." Adam looked a little sad."You know, Wyatt was married right out of high school. Judy was his high school sweetheart. She had the same name as my Mom does and they were a lot alike. Judy was such a sweet girl. They dated for years and got married after graduation. They were married for 6 years when Judy had an aneurysm burst in her head. She was on life support for over a month when the doctors finally told Wyatt that Judy was brain dead and wouldn't recover. I thought Wyatt would never get over it enough to live a normal life. It was really bad there for a while. A year later, he was elected Sheriff...he had been a deputy when he and Judy were married. I think his job saved his life. It gave him something to occupy his mind. I still worry about him sometimes and I try to keep up with how things are going for him."

"Wow, Adam. I had no idea. That is so sad. I am glad I thought about inviting him to dinner tomorrow night. Maybe we can all get together more often after these horrible murders and thefts are solved. I hate to think of Wyatt being lonely and depressed." Landry choked up.

She stood up and said, "Well, I guess we better get back inside since Zep ran back in the open sliding glass doors while we were talking. I am not sure about him yet and don't want him to tear anything up. I have truly been amazed at how good he is when he is alone here during the day."

They got up to go in and Adam said, "By the way, what is that on the side of your face? Did you get hurt?" Landry rolled her eyes and waved her hand, "Nope. Just a little mishap at the Takeout King today. You don't even want to know." Adam looked curious but didn't say anymore.

When they got back inside, Zep was in the den chewing on a toy. Landry refilled their coffee cups and they sat in the den and watched a 30 minute game show. When it was over, Adam said that he needed to be getting home. Landry could tell that he really had had a tough day. She saw him out and then headed to the kitchen to straighten up and wash out the coffee pot. That done, she went to the den and turned off the tv. She picked up Zep and walked around and made sure everything was locked up. After she washed her face and put on her pj's, she and Zep got in the bed. She said a special prayer for Mr. Larson. She hoped that he would heal up soon and be able to return to the building. She read a book until she fell asleep.

Chapter 14

The next morning, Landry got dressed and took Zep on a morning walk. He loved being outside and the exercise was good for her. During their walk, she thought about the murders and thefts and decided that the two crimes had to be related. On the way back to the apartment building, her phone rang. It was Wyatt. "Hey, Landry. First all, thanks for the invite to dinner tonight. I am really looking forward to it. Please don't go to any trouble, though. Anything other than takeout will seem like a gourmet meal to me."

Landry laughed and said, "I think I can do a little better than that. We are so glad you are joining us. I love to cook, just not for only me."

"Sounds awesome. Look, I wanted to fill you in on a few things. First, we got the DNA results back from Melodie's crime scene. It doesn't match any on file or any of the ones we have taken of our suspects. But, the interesting thing is that the foreign DNA from under Melodie's fingernails is from a male. The DNA from Fred's scene was from a female. We have two different killers to find. This dang case gets more complicated as we get more information. Also, for some reason, Scat's old truck has gone missing. My deputies said he has stopped driving it to the Purple Cactus and that he has been driving Portia's car when they see him around town. They saw him walking one day and asked him where his truck was. He basically told them it was none of their business and to leave him alone unless he was under arrest. We put a BOLO out for the truck and I hope when it is located we can understand why he stopped driving it and where it has been. I have a feeling that truck has a story to tell us."

"That is very strange." Landry sounded puzzled. "Oh, Wyatt, I just remembered something. Tonight at dinner remember to ask Adam about the couple of times he saw Fred driving what may have been that same truck. Adam was on the way out to his Aunt and Uncle's farm and said that Fred was with different people each time but was driving a truck that sounds very similar to that one.

"Sure thing. The other thing I wanted to say is that I am very sorry about Mr. Larson, Landry. I checked this morning and he is still in the ICU. I hope the old man makes it. He always seemed like a good person to me."

"I hope so, too. Will he face any charges, Wyatt? I know he ran a stoplight."

"Probably just a charge for running the light. He ran slap into a huge garbage truck. Mr. Larson's car was totaled and, well, you know how beat up his body is. The truck was barely dented. The owner of the garbage company said that he knew Mr. Larson pretty well and that he would not file any charges against him if Larson agreed to never drive on the roads again. I think the guy is more worried about Larson's well being than anything else. We will have to file charges for running the light and reckless endangerment, but he won't go to jail if that is what you are asking."

Landry blew out the breath she was holding. "Thank the Lord for that. I just hope that he can recover from his injuries and live a good quality of life after this. Listen, Wyatt, I have to run now but I will see you tonight for dinner. Have a good day."

"You, too." Wyatt hung up.

Landry went back to the apartment and grabbed a yogurt and some coffee for her breakfast. She ate on the balcony and then settled Zep into the den. She also took the bandaid off of her face since it was healing up and there was no blood anymore. When she got back to the lobby, Lisa was at her desk and just hanging up the phone. "Hey, Landry. That was Mr. Larson's son. He said that his Dad is not out of the woods yet but he is off the ventilator. They are hoping he can be moved to a regular room tomorrow. He has several broken bones and had to have surgery. His son is hopeful that it will all heal and he won't have to go through any more surgeries. When he is moved to a regular room, I will order flowers from all of us and have them delivered."

Landry nodded her head and thanked Lisa for the information. "He is very blessed to be doing as well as he is. His age will probably hinder him a little in his recovery but he seems like a determined man."

"He does. Oh, and Mr. Harcourt called. He said he is 'reluctantly approving' the security cameras." Lisa rolled her eyes. "He said since we were robbed of a valuable painting that he thinks the building does need more security. Landry if you don't want to say, I completely understand, but I just have to ask. Does Mr. Harcourt control all of your money? What I mean is, do you have to ask his permission to buy clothes, groceries or other things?"

Landry laughed. "I don't mind telling you, Lisa. No, he doesn't. He controls the money that is generated by this building, meaning the money made from rent, and the money generated by the bookstore. I have my personal banking account for the actual money I inherited from Aunt Tildie and my money that I had when I moved here. I had saved up quite a bit working at the Library since I was renting a small house and was single. So, no, he doesn't control all aspects of my finances and I am happy about that. Plus, he only controls it for a year. After that, I will probably hire a Financial Advisor that won't have complete control of the business finances and decisions but will be there if I need advice."

"Sorry, Landry. I realize that is none of my business but I was feeling pretty bad for you if Mr. Harcourt was telling you what to do with every penny you own. He is even hard to deal with on the phone when he leaves you a message with me." Lisa smiled.

"Lisa, could you call Mr. Mayhew and let him know that he is cleared to get the security cameras installed." She reached in her purse and pulled out her phone. "I have a list of where I want each camera and I will send it to your phone. I know he is out of town a lot, so ask him to please let you know when the installation will take place." Lisa nodded and Landry walked out to the sidewalk after telling Garrett good morning.

Her first stop was at the bookstore. "Good morning,

Ms. Millie." she yelled as she walked in the door. Ms. Millie stuck her head out of the small storage room at the back. "Hey there, Landry. Lenny and Carl just got here a few minutes ago. They are moving the stuff to the big storage room. I sure hope you are planning to spruce this room up. Looks like a bunch of pigs are living here right now."

Landry laughed. Ms. Millie never held back on her opinions. "I sure am, Ms. Millie. The guys here are going to paint the walls bright white for us and then I am going to see if I can get somebody to paint a couple of cute murals on the walls. Then, I will get carpet installed and you and I are going to scour thrift stores and yard sales for kid furniture to go in there."

"I like going to yard sales. I guess we might have to recruit your boyfriend to take us around in his big SUV. That Bug of yours won't hold even one piece of furniture and my car isn't much bigger." Ms. Millie had a twinkle in her eye.

"Ms. Millie, you know Adam is not my boyfriend. Nothing of the sort. We are friends and I am sure he will be glad to help us out." Landry felt her face getting hot and turned away from Ms. Millie until she could get her embarrassment under control. She turned back around and said, "I also wanted to ask you something else. Since it is almost summer and Jenna will be graduating, is she planning on still working here? If she is, I might switch her hours around to include working all day with you. That would give her a full time job and more pay. Of course, if she is leaving to go away to college, I guess that wouldn't work for her."

Ms. Millie looked at her. "I am not sure what that child is planning. I overheard her mentioning to Maisy the other day that she might just do online studies for the first couple of years since her parents don't have much money. If that is what she is planning, I know she would love the extra hours and pay to save up for on campus learning down the road. You need to talk to her. I would love the extra help while I am here…it would keep me from running from the office in the back when I am doing paperwork to the front when a customer comes in. I ain't as young as I used to be, ya know."

"I know." Landry smiled and patted her on the shoulder. "How are sales going, Ms. Millie? Are we still making a profit after all the expenses are paid?"

"Oh, yes. You know that we order all of the books for the schools in town, don't you? Tildie managed to get that contract when the district decided to outsource the ordering of books to lighten the load on the office help at the schools. They had to cut back on positions there during the summer. It works out good for them and great for us. We also have quite a few Moms who homeschool, especially the ones whose husbands travel for work. The women homeschool so that they can pick up and travel whenever they want and the kids are still learning. We will have an influx of orders for books for the new school session very soon. And, of course, as the only bookstore in town, we sell tons of regular reading books, cookbooks, how to books and so on. I keep a count of everything we sell and also the expenses. I still write everything longhand in a journal. We are making a very good profit here, Landry."

Landry felt the relief flow through her. "That is wonderful, Ms. Millie. I am so grateful to you for doing all of this. Even if Jenna doesn't want full time hours, I will get you someone in here that will work full time. That way, you won't have to work so hard to get everything done." She hugged Ms. Millie and told her that the two of them would get together soon and order the books for the Children's Room. They already had a section of kids books but Landry wanted to add to it. She told the maintenance guys goodbye and left the bookstore.

She needed to go to the grocery store to pick up the things she needed for dinner tonight. She also wanted to pick up some ingredients she needed to make a couple of pies to take to the farm on Sunday. Adam had said she didn't have to bring anything but, like every woman from the South, she never showed up to eat at someone's house empty handed. She realized that she had written the list of things she needed down on paper instead of putting it in her phone, so she ran back across the street to grab it.

When she stepped into her apartment, she saw something on the floor. Another note. Landry first went to make sure that Zep was still there. He was in the den sleeping. She went back to the living room and used a napkin to pick up the note.

PLEASE STAY OUT OF THIS INVESTIGATION. YOU COULD BE HURT.

Landry sighed and got a baggie from the kitchen and put the note in it. She grabbed her grocery list and put both items in her purse and went back to the lobby.

She asked Lisa and Garrett if they had noticed anyone out of the ordinary come into the building. They both said no. "Just the usual residents and employees so far today." Garrett said.

Lisa asked, "Is something wrong, Landry?"

Landry told her no and turned and went to the garage. Before she went to the grocery store, she had to make a trip to the Sheriff's Department so she wanted to drive her car.

When she showed Wyatt the new note he told her that they didn't get any foreign DNA off of the first one. "Whoever is leaving them must be wearing gloves. The only DNA we got was yours. Remember we swabbed both you and Adam the day of the murder to rule out your DNA from the crime scene."

"I asked Garrett and Lisa if anyone other than the employees or residents of the building had come in today. They both said no and that one of them was in the Lobby the entire time. This is so puzzling to me. The only thing that even makes sense is that one of the residents is putting it under my door without having to enter the Lobby. That frightens me, Wyatt." She started twirling her ring on her finger. She had a bad feeling in her stomach and was thinking so hard, her head was pounding.

Wyatt noticed that she was nervous but he thought it better not to mention it. Instead, he tried to comfort her as best he could. "Landry, I know this is getting to you. It is getting to all of us here, too. We want to figure this out before anybody else gets hurt or worse. Please just be aware of your surroundings and be as careful as possible. I will see if there is DNA on this note, but the chances are slim."

Landry rubbed the sides of her temples and got up to leave. "Thanks, Wyatt. I have some errands to run but I will see you tonight." She asked the desk deputy if she could get a cup of coffee to go. She was hoping the caffeine would help her head. When she got to her car, she pulled a protein bar out of her purse and ate it with the coffee. Feeling a little better, she drove away.

Chapter 15

Landry's first stop was at the Art Gallery. She went in and looked around. She noticed a very well dressed woman with what she could tell was expensive and extravagant jewelry. She assumed this was Sylvia Weathers, the owner. She walked over and the woman asked if she needed some help.

"I am Landry Burke. Tildie Mayweather's niece. How do you do?" Landry offered her hand to the woman.

"Of course." The woman shook her hand and said, "I heard that you had inherited Miss Tildie's estate. I am so sorry about your loss. She was a wonderful woman and client. I miss seeing her. I am also sorry that I haven't been to welcome you to our town. I should have done that a long time ago. I just get so involved in the Gallery and all that it entails. My name is Sylvia Weathers and I own this Gallery." She waved her arm around like the woman on the game show that shows all the wonderful prizes.

Landry took a step back. Her anxiety caused her to feel claustrophobic sometimes and Sylvia was standing a little too close for her liking. Then she said to Sylvia, "It is perfectly alright. I know how owning businesses can take over your time. I understand that my Aunt purchased some paintings from you."

"Yes, she did. She absolutely loved magnolias and I was always on the lookout for the most prominent paintings that showcased them. I also helped with framing all of her paintings, whether she purchased them from me or not, so that they would all match. She wanted the Event Room at Magnolia Place to feature them in all their glory. I was so sorry to hear of one of them being stolen. That and a murder in the building must have you on edge, dear."

"Yes, it does. I am hoping that the painting can be recovered when the Sheriff's Department finds out who took it." Landry answered.

Sylvia turned her head to one side, "Do they have any leads?"

"Not that I am aware of." Landry decided at that moment that she would not reveal any details that Wyatt had entrusted her with. It was good of him to keep her and Adam informed because they had found Fred's body in her building. She knew he trusted them to keep the details to themselves.

"Well, I certainly hope they find the painting." Sylvia looked solemn as she said, "You know, that was one of the most expensive paintings that I procured for any of my clients. An original and we were very lucky to find it for Miss Tildie. But, each and every time she asked me to help her locate one that she had her heart set on, I worked diligently to do just that. As I mentioned, she was a valued client but even more so a cherished friend. I have top notch security here but it still makes me nervous to hear about paintings being stolen. As a Gallery owner, that is one of my biggest fears. Now, can I help you with something in the Gallery today, Landry?"

"Oh, no not today. I do have a question though. I am

creating a Children's Room at the bookstore and I would love to hire a local artist to do a couple of murals for me. Someone suggested I ask you since you are the center of the art world in this town."

"Actually, I do have a name for you. Chloe Duncan. She is the art teacher at the elementary school and she has won many contests for her art. She enters at least one a year all over the country. She is an amazing artist and I know of at least one mural she has done for an expectant Mom in town. The Mom wanted a particular themed mural and Chloe knocked it out of the park. You can contact the office at the school and ask them to have her contact you about doing a mural. I know she would be thrilled to have her art featured at the bookstore."

"Thank you so much. That sounds perfect and I will get in touch with her." Landry thought for a second. "If I ever decide to update the pictures in the Lobby of Magnolia Place, I will contact you. Thank you for all of your help." Sylvia looked pleased with that and Landry lingered a while longer to look at the artwork and handmade fig in the Gallery.

When Landry left the Art Gallery, she headed to the grocery store. She got out her list and started shopping. Cubed steak, fresh corn on the cob, fresh asparagus, some round snack crackers, chopped nuts, cool whip and coconut. Those were the items on the list for tonight's dinner and the pies for the farm. She had everything else she needed in the apartment already. She went to another aisle and added a pack of whole grain waffles, a large jar of peanut butter and some cereal to her cart. She checked out and went back home and carried her purchases upstairs. She didn't need a cart from the garage since she hadn't bought that much. When she got them all put up, she looked at the time. She still had plenty of time before she had to start cooking, so she put Zep's collar and leash on and they went to the park.

They were walking through the park and Landry was marveling at how well Zep behaved. She hadn't had any problems with him so far. He ate well, played hard, used his puppy pads and slept great at night. Since she had started leaving the tv on for him, he wasn't even whining anymore when she left the apartment. He was walking on his leash and stopped every now and then to roll and tumble or to sniff at something on the ground. It was a gorgeous day.

All of a sudden a cat came running at full speed right past them. Zep's ears stood straight up and he lunged toward where the cat was going. Landry was taken by surprise and the leash flew out of her hand. She stared as the cat, Zep and the leash almost disappeared before her eyes. The cat had made a sharp right turn and Zep had followed suit. Landry hit the ground running as fast as she could. She got to the place where the animals had turned and she stopped in her tracks.

The cat was somehow on the top of a pineapple statue in the middle of a water fountain. Zep had jumped up on the low brick wall surrounding the fountain. He kept raising his paw up over the water but didn't try to jump in, thank goodness. Landy walked slow and steady to try to get close enough to grab the leash. Just as she almost had it, the crazy cat jumped down from the top of the statue and landed right on Landry's head. She screamed and that caused Zep to jump and lose his balance. He fell right into the water from the fountain. When Landry finally got the cat untangled from her unruly hair, it took off like a bolt of lightning across the park. Landry turned around and saw Zep. He had gotten to the middle of the water where it was shallow enough that it didn't reach his head.

"Come on, Zep. Mommy's got you. Just come this way a little so that I can reach you." Landry tried to coax him. Zep was frozen right where he was. He was not moving a muscle. He could have been a statue himself. "Please, Zep. Please come to Mommy." Landry pleaded. The standoff lasted for what seemed to Landry to be hours but in reality was only a few minutes. She looked around to see if there was anyone else within shouting distance to help her. Nope. Of course not.

She finally settled on the fact that she was going to have to go in at least enough to reach the leash and pull Zep over to where she was. She took off her shoes and stuck her foot in the fountain and, for it to be getting close to summer, the water was freezing. She looked up at Zep and he was shivering. She wasn't sure if it was from the cold water or fear but, at that moment, she made a decision. She got in the fountain and walked over to where the end of the leash was floating in the water. She grabbed it and that is when Zep decided that he was not afraid now that Landry was in there with him. He ran around the base of the statue and jerked on the leash. Landry fell face first in the water. She got up and grabbed the leash. Since she was already ringing wet, she chased Zep until she caught him. She was getting them both out of the fountain when, of course, several people showed up. The kids in the group were laughing; their parents were saying things like, "what in the world?" or "what is she doing?". Landry could only imagine what she looked like. She went over and picked up her shoes and looked at the gawkers. "Beautiful day, isn't it?"

When she got back to the apartment building. Lisa just stared at her. Landry waved her off and started to head for the elevator when someone else walked in the door. She turned and saw a gorgeous woman that looked like a movie star. Long brown hair with dark brown eyes and olive skin. She was wearing a bright pink dress that barely covered her and had on the highest heels Landry had ever seen. Her lipstick matched her dress perfectly.

Lisa looked at the woman and said, "What do you want, Pam? I already told you that I am not interested in selling my folks' home."

Landry was curious and she walked back over to Lisa's desk. She nodded her head at Pam and said, "Hello. I am Landry Burke. I am the owner of the building. Could we help you with something?"

Lisa shook her head and said, "Don't be nice to her, Landry. You will regret it. This is Pam Rivers. She and Adam used to date. She is a realtor here in town and stalks those of us that have properties she would like to sell."

Pam looked offended and said, "That is not true, Lisa. How is Adam, by the way? I thought I might ask him to go to dinner one night. Old times sake, you know? We had some very good times together."

That got Landry's attention. She had never heard about any of Adam's exes. That is the moment she realized how she must look. Soaking wet, dirty and carrying a dog that was also wet and stinky. Just perfect, especially since Pam looked like she belonged on the cover of a fashion magazine.

"He is seeing someone else, Pam. He moved on quickly after you, which was a surprise to noone. Again, what are you doing here?!" Lisa sounded disgusted. Landry wondered why Lisa disliked this woman so much that she had just lied to her about Adam seeing someone else.

"For your information, I am here to see Diane Huffman, the Assistant Bank Manager. She is looking to purchase a home and get out of her apartment. I am helping her with that search. Now, if you don't mind. Please let her know I am here for our appointment." Pam sashayed over to a chair and sat. She had never even acknowledged Landry's introduction.

Landry turned and got on the elevator. Rude woman, she thought. Once she got them both back home, she immediately put Zep in the tub. She towel dried him and let him run to dry the rest of the way while she got a shower, pulled her hair up and threw on some thin sweatpants, a t-shirt and socks. At least it was just Adam and Wyatt for dinner tonight. She couldn't have fixed herself up if she had to. She checked on Zep...he was asleep in the den. "Well," she thought to herself, "I guess we know he likes to chase cats."

She looked at the clock and saw that all of her "extra time" was up. It was time to start dinner. She put food and water down for Zep in case he woke up and then started a pot of coffee. She was still chilled from that icy water but knew that she would warm up when she turned the stove on. She got out her phone and put on some 80's music to listen to while she cooked.

She had the cubed steak seasoned and floured and when the oil was hot, she put it in the cast iron skillet. While that was frying, she put on a pot of rice and shucked and washed the fresh corn. She dropped the ears in a pot of boiling water with salt and butter. She turned the meat and then washed off the asparagus and put it in a double boiler to steam. She took the cooked cubed steak out of the pan and put in another batch. She had a feeling that the guys would be hungry tonight. She would get all of this done and keep it warm in the oven while she made the gravy and sweet tea. For now she flipped the meat and went out on the balcony to sit until it was time to take it up. She liked cooking cubed steak since it didn't take long and the gravy made from it was delicious.

As she sat outside, she began to think about how fortunate she was. Not just that she had inherited a good deal from Aunt Tildie but that she had been able to come to a new town and make a life for herself with new friends, new challenges and new blessings. Even with the murders and thefts still unsolved, she honestly felt like she belonged and that she had people she could count on to be there for her. It was a great feeling.

She had called the school earlier and spoke with Chloe Duncan, who was more than excited to do the murals for the Children's Room. They discussed what Landry's ideas were and she told Chloe to just go for it and do whatever she thought was best. Then, Chloe told her about one of the older local daycares that was closing and was having a yard sale tomorrow. She told Landry that she knew they would have lots of children's tables and chairs as well as other things for sale. Chloe said they were having it in the empty lot next to the daycare and gave Landry the directions to get there. Landry thanked her profusely and then called Ms. Millie and asked her if she could go tomorrow. Ms. Millie said yes, but again said that Landry should probably ask Adam if he would take them in his big SUV. "You know that little toy car of yours won't hold much." Ms. Millie said. Landry shook her head at the description of her beloved car but agreed to do what Ms. Millie requested.

She went back to the kitchen and took the meat out and put it on the platter with the first ones. She put that in the warm oven and moved the pan to the other eye until she was ready to make the gravy, then checked on the vegetables. Everything looked good. She hummed to the song playing in the background. She loved music from the 70's and 80's. She always felt like she was born in the wrong era. She was 28 years old but she had an old soul.

She loved anything vintage and she even liked the old black and white movies or the reruns of sitcoms from days gone by.

She heard "tap, tap, tap" on the floor. She looked down and there was Zep. He looked up at her and whined very softly. "Oh, Zep. I'm not mad. You were just trying to have some fun. I would appreciate it if you could remember that my hair is not meant to be wet in public places, though." She bent down to scratch his head and he licked her face. Landry said lovingly, "We are perfect for each other."

Just then, she heard a knock on the door. She started to wonder who it was until she glanced at the clock. 6pm…time had gotten away from her. Thank goodness she had at least been cooking while she was daydreaming.

She asked who was at the door and she heard Adam say, "Just one of your dinner dates for tonight." She laughed and let him in. He handed her a meat and cheese platter. "I didn't have time to whip anything up, so I thought I would bring this for an appetizer."

"Thanks. That's great. Say, I met someone in the lobby today that you know. Pam Rivers?" Landry said casually.

Adam rolled his eyes. "I sure hope you didn't have to be around her long. I dated her for about two seconds. I have no idea what I was thinking. She was like a bulldog and kept asking me to go out. I had a weak moment and said yes. That woman was horrible, Landry! She hated all my friends and family and said awful things about them. She complained all the time about everything. My clothes, my hair, where we went out to eat. I am telling you, I am so glad to be rid of all that. Why was she here in the lobby? I know she and Lisa despise each other." He walked over to pet Zep on the head.

"Seems one of our residents is looking to purchase a home. Pam is showing her some that are available." Landry said as she walked back into the kitchen. She couldn't resist adding, "Oh, and Pam told Lisa that she is going to ask you out to dinner soon."

She could hear Adam making a gagging noise. "Not gonna happen. I got out of that mess and I am never going back. Nope. You can take that to the bank. End of subject." He said fervently.

Landry smiled to herself and thought, "That relationship must have been awful for him."

"I love your taste in music." Adam said as he listened to a song that was playing.. "Thanks," she said. "I have eclectic tastes, actually. I mostly love 70's and 80's rock but I also like some Blues, Jazz, Country…pretty much everything depending on my mood." She started swaying to the music in the kitchen as she made the tea and took the plastic wrap off of the platter. Adam sat on the couch in the living room with Zep in his lap. There was a knock at the door and Adam got up to let Wyatt in.

"Hey man." Wyatt said. "It sure is nice to be here with friends, music, a dog and food. So much going on right as I walk in and I love it. It gets pretty boring being by myself. Hey Landry," he shouted to the kitchen, "I brought an apple pie. I mean, I didn't make it or anything but I've had one of these before and they are pretty good."

Landry walked out of the kitchen and grinned. "Wyatt, you saved the day. I didn't even realize that I had nothing for dessert until you said apple pie. Thank you so much. Come on in and have some of these appetizers that Adam brought."

Wyatt said, "Don't mind if I do." He walked back to the living room, sat down and started talking with Adam. Landry made them glasses of iced tea and grabbed a few crackers, meat and cheese before she went back into the kitchen to finish making dinner.

She was almost finished with the gravy when Wyatt yelled from the living room, "I sent that second note to the lab to see if we could extract any DNA, Landry. Like I said, though, I don't think we will find anything." She heard Adam pipe in, "Second note? You got another one?" She quickly put the cubed steak into the gravy and put the top on it for a few minutes.

She walked into the living room, "Oops, sorry Adam. I was so busy cooking when you got here that I forgot to mention it." She proceeded to tell him what the note said and that Lisa and Garrett didn't see anyone come into the building when it was put under her door.

"This makes me very nervous, Landry. I wonder who it could be?" Landry shrugged her shoulders and shook her head. "Dinner is ready, guys. Come on in the kitchen."

They all made their plates, Adam said the blessing and they all dove in. Both of the guys oohed and awed over the food. They kept telling Landry how wonderful it was to have a good old southern dinner. She had some pickled beets and cut up onions on the table and they ate that, too. It made her happy to see them devouring the meal. Wyatt ate four pieces of cubed steak and two helpings of rice and gravy, along with everything else. Adam stopped at two pieces of steak but ate two helpings of the asparagus. When they were done, the guys put the dishes in the dishwasher and even put the leftovers in the fridge and washed the pots. While they did that, Landry started a fresh pot of coffee and held Zep and snuggled him for a few minutes. The guys had been playing with him while she had been cooking.

When the guys were done, all of them got a piece of apple pie and a cup of coffee and headed out to the balcony. It was a gorgeous night and very comfortable. Landry had put fresh food and water down for Zep and when he was full, he rolled around and grunted which was a sure sign that he was one happy puppy.

"This is nice." Adam said. Landry and Wyatt both agreed.

Landry spoke up, "Honestly, this is the first time since college that I have felt like I belonged, except for my best friend, Annie, back in Bent Branch. She and I are like sisters and I miss her so much. I feel like you two and Lisa are my real friends here in Bobwhite Mountain and that I don't have to go through everything in my life alone. I am so comfortable around y'all and my anxiety has gotten so much better. I mean, I still have panic attacks from time to time but I don't feel so isolated. I feel like I can be myself instead of hiding my feelings and other things about my life. Does that even make sense?"

"It does to me." Wyatt looked straight ahead with a solemn look on his face and said. "Since Judy died, I have pretty much isolated myself from everybody except for Adam here. It's like I didn't want to see all the sad looks and the 'poor Wyatt' faces. At the office, I laid the law down and told them straight out not to treat me that way. Of course, at first everybody in town truly was sorry and I was still pretty much in shock but, after so long, I just couldn't be reminded of it every day by every person I spoke to. Don't get me wrong, it's always on my mind. It took years for me to not think about it every second of every day. Now that I feel that I can move on with my life, I don't want to be reminded of the absolute worst time that I ever went through. Does that make sense?"

Adam looked at them and nodded. "Both situations make perfect sense to me. Since high school, I have had women see me for just my looks. They pester me, try to get my attention, and want to date me. I don't want any of them. I mean, yeah, I want to get married and have a family one day but to someone who isn't superficial. That gets old very fast. I want someone who makes fun of the parts of me that aren't perfect. I have flaws just like everybody else but, so far, none of the women I have met have even bothered to try to find them. They want an attorney who is handsome and what they consider wealthy. I want someone who is down to earth and quirky just like the real me; someone who wants a family and has their own goals in life. Wyatt is the best friend I have ever had. He rags on me and never lets me get complacent. He never minds pointing out my faults and I am thankful for it. It keeps me grounded. Does that make sense?"

They all got real quiet and then busted out laughing all together. They almost fell out of the chairs. "Man, we are a sorry bunch of misfits." laughed Wyatt. "We better be glad we found each other...nobody else would have us for friends."

Adam and Landry were still laughing. It was a great night for all of them, especially Wyatt. He couldn't remember the last time he felt so good and at ease around people. He looked out at the mountainside and said a silent prayer thanking God for reminding him that, even though Judy was gone, he was still here. He felt more alive in that moment, with those people, than he had in years.

And, that's when his phone beeped. "Dang it.," he yelled into the night air. "One night...just one night without work calling would be perfect." Adam and Landry looked at each other.

"What?" Wyatt snapped when he answered the phone. He listened for a minute, thanked the caller for letting him know and then hung up.

"Something bad, Wyatt?" Adam asked.

"That was Police Chief Edmunds over in Wrigley Springs. Seems they just got called to the home of State Senator Maines that lives over there. He and his wife just got back from Washington, DC. They were there for a few days for some events. When they got back home, they discovered their house had been broken into. The robbers went in through the basement window in the backyard. Guess what was missing?"

"A painting." Landry almost whispered the answer.

"Yep." Wyatt nodded his head. "One that they had commissioned from a prominent artist they had met in Washington a few years back. Of course, they don't have security cameras and nobody was home at the time since they value their privacy and the Senator's wife, Camille, prefers to not have any staff. Their kids are grown now and she doesn't work outside of the home and is still young enough to handle things herself."

"This is getting crazy. Murders and thefts. In all my life here, I have not ever seen crime this bad in Bobwhite Mountain." Adam shook his head.

"Well, guys. I am going to have to hit the road. Landry, the dinner was amazing. I really appreciate that and I also had the best time I have had in years just hanging out with both of you." Wyatt stood.

Adam and Landry walked him inside and said their goodbyes. When he left, they both walked back to the den and saw Zep laying on the couch. He popped his head up when they came in and started jumping. Adam looked at Landry, "I think I will take him for a quick walk and then I will be heading home, too. It's been a very long day."

"Speaking of that, I have never asked you where you live, Adam. Is it close by?" Landry asked him.

"Not too far." he replied as he was putting the leash on Zep. "I bought a townhome in one of the newer gated communities here. It's about halfway up the mountain.

That's why I drive that big four wheel drive. It can get pretty dangerous on the mountain roads in the winter with all the snow and ice we usually get."

Landry nodded and said, "Oh, that reminds me. Ms. Millie and I need to go to a yard sale tomorrow. Chloe Duncan told me that a local daycare is closing up shop and that we can probably find some children's furniture and a few other things for the Children's Room I am creating at the bookstore. My car would hardly hold anything that we might find so I was wondering if you would be interested in taking us in your SUV? They are starting the sale at 10am tomorrow."

"Absolutely. I love going to yard sales, anyway. Never know what you might find. Kinda fun." He turned and told Zep to follow him.

When the two of them got back, Adam thanked Landry again and left to go home. Landry locked up, put on her pj's, and turned everything off. She and Zep settled into bed and she turned the tv volume on low and was watching an old sitcom. She started rubbing her feet together under the comforter and yawned. "Time for us to go to sleep, Zep." She turned and heard the puppy snoring very softly.

Chapter 16

After Landry got up and grabbed some coffee, she took Zep for a morning walk. She was careful to not go near the park today since she didn't want a repeat of the cat and dog show. When they got back, she had just finished a bowl of cereal when she got a message on her phone. It was Lisa reminding her of the Pink Hat Ladies event that was tonight at 7pm. Lisa said that Orvis had started his weekend work for them today and would be there until 9pm. The events were scheduled for two hours and Orvis had said he wouldn't go up to his apartment until all of the ladies were gone and he made sure the Event Room was locked up. Lisa said that Mrs. Cartwright had hired a local maid to come in and clean up behind them on Sunday afternoon.

Landry decided to go over to the bookstore and check in. She wasn't sure which of the girls was working this Saturday but she wanted to check on the progress of the Children's Room. When she got to the Lobby, she noticed Orvis saying goodbye to Richard and Nelda Harris, residents of the 3rd floor. Richard was the Youth Pastor and Music Director at the church Landry attended and his wife, Nelda, was a kindergarten aide at the elementary school. They walked out and Landry went up to Orvis.

"I hope you will enjoy working for us on the weekends, Orvis."

"Oh, I know I will, Miss Burke. I need the extra money since working at a car dealership just during the week doesn't pay much.," he looked grateful for getting this job.

"Do you sell cars there, Orvis?" Landry asked.

"No, ma'am. I work in the Service Department."

Landry asked him why he lived here in Bobwhite Mountain when he worked in Wrigley Springs. He explained that he grew up in Bobwhite Mountain and had worked there when he rented the apartment. When the place where he worked closed up, he found the job in Wrigley Springs but didn't want to live there. His friends and family were all here.

Landry said that made sense to her and told him she was going out for a little bit but that her cell phone number was taped to the Lobby Assistant's desk if he needed her for an emergency. She went across the street to the bookstore.

It was busy already. They opened at 8am on Saturday. Maisy was the clerk there today. There were several customers buying books, one was asking about the apple cinnamon potpourri that filled the store with a wonderful scent. They sold it by the bag and Maisy pointed to it as she was ringing up another customer. Landry heard a noise in the back of the bookstore and went to the small storage room that had been cleared out. There, she found Chloe Duncan working on one of the murals. "Wow. I didn't know you would start so fast. I just spoke with you yesterday afternoon." Landry sounded shocked.

"I had time today to get started and I already had some of the colors of paint I needed for the project. Right now, I am sketching the drawing on the wall. If I have time, I will begin the painting process. If not, I will come in on afternoons after school next week to work on it. This is my passion. I love doing murals, especially ones that are aimed towards children."

Landry thanked her again for being so prompt and went back to the front of the bookstore. The customers had thinned out and Maisy was checking out the last one in the store. When she was done, she looked at Landry. "Hey Boss Lady. How's things going?"

Landry smiled and said, "Fine, Maisy. How about with you?"

Maisy looked like she was thinking about that question too hard. "Well, see, it's like this. I love to play sports, read, get good grades and work here. I also like to play with my baby brother. That all makes me happy. I know I am only in 9th grade but I am supposed to be in 10th. I was very sick in 1st grade and had to repeat that year."

Landry wondered where in the world this conversation was going until Maisy finally got to her point.

"You see, Boss Lady," Maisy said very seriously, "I kinda worry about Jenna. She is graduating high school this year and still has no idea what she is going to do. I mean, she hasn't applied to any colleges and that's fine. Lots of people go straight to work after high school or even go to school at night while working. But, Jenna just seems a little lost about it all. I also know she was asked to Prom and said she turned the guy down because she didn't want to burden her parents with the cost of a dress, shoes and other things she would need. That is just sad to me. I offered to "lend" her the money and she could pay me back 1.00 at a time from her paycheck. If she never paid me back, I wouldn't care but I know she is proud so I presented it to her that way. She said thanks but no. I just worry about her, that's all."

Landry thought that was the sweetest thing ever. Maisy was still very young herself but she was way more smarter and caring than some people twice her age. She was ashamed that she thought that Maisy was the last person she expected this caring attitude from. "You know what, Maisy? I can't help Jenna decide what she wants to do with her life…that is her decision. But, if she decides to go to work full time, that can be arranged here at the bookstore. Also, just between you and me, I happen to know that my church has a 'Secret Closet' for any girls who want to go to Prom and can't afford to purchase what they need. I helped to arrange the closet last week and there are some gorgeous dresses, shoes, purses, hair accessories, all kinds of nice things. It is all free. Please mention this to Jenna and tell her you will go over there with her if she still wants to go to prom. Please don't tell her I told you about it…I don't want to embarrass her. I am very proud of you Maisy for worrying about your friend."

Just then, Landry thought of something else and she stuck her index finger in the air. "Oh, and Maisy, you might want to tell her another detail about the Secret Closet. You see, a church about 100 miles away does the same thing in their town. Then, someone from our church and someone from theirs meet about halfway between and exchange all of the items collected. That way, nobody has to be embarrassed by someone coming up to them and saying, 'That was my dress year before last.' or 'So and so wore that to Prom last year.' The churches pay to have all of the dresses cleaned and they even have those plastic bags over them from the dry cleaners. It is just like shopping from a store, but it is all free."

"Thanks, Boss Lady. I like Jenna and she has always been very good to me, especially since she is a Senior and I am just a Freshman. Sometimes Seniors can act all high and mighty, ya know?" Maisy shook her head.

Landry said she did know and that she was glad that Jenna wasn't like that. She told Maisy to let her know how the conversation about Prom went with Jenna and gave Maisy a piece of paper with the Church's address, although Maisy said she knew right where it was.

Landry went back across the street to Magnolia Place to get her purse and wait on Adam to pick her up to go to the yard sale. He was picking Ms. Millie up first and then they would swing by for Landry. When Adam pulled up in front of the building, Ms. Millie was in the back seat. "Don't you want to ride shotgun, Ms. Millie?" Landry asked as she was getting in.

"No, I do not. The last time I did that, YOU went and found a body. I am hoping that Adam won't be so careless as to do that to me. Just in case, I want to sit in the back in case I need to hide from another bad guy." Landry and Adam smiled at each other and Adam shook his head before he pulled onto the road.

When they stopped at the stoplight, Landry saw something out of the corner of her eye. She turned and saw the beat up, old blue truck that had been at the trailer. "Adam. There it is. The truck that Wyatt said nobody could find." She pointed out the window excitedly.

Adam looked in the direction she pointed in just as the truck was speeding off. "Landry, that is definitely the truck I saw Fred in that one time. Call Wyatt and let him know."

As Landry was dialing, she heard something from the backseat. "Lord, please, I am begging you don't do this to me again. I am an old woman and these things are gonna kill me." It was Ms. Millie praying…from the floorboard where she was hiding.

Adam looked around and saw her just as he was pulling off from the redlight. "Get up, Ms. Millie. I am not going to follow the truck. They have a big head start on us and we aren't armed. I'm not sure who was in that truck but I don't feel like getting shot at today." he said as Landry was talking to Wyatt.

"Praise Jesus. I knew you were a smart man, Adam. It seems like everytime I get in a car with Landry, the criminals show up."

Landry hung up with Wyatt after he said he was putting his deputies on it. "Two times, Ms. Millie, two times." Landry moaned.

"Chile, how many times have I been in a car with you? How many?" Ms. Millie yelled.

"Two." Landry said meekly.

"I rest my case." Ms. Millie said smugly.

They got to the empty field beside the daycare. It looked like a huge crowd was there. They were selling drinks and snacks and even had a big bouncy house for the kids. There were fishing games, duck games and all sorts of things. The lady who owned the daycare came up to them and welcomed them to the yard sale. Landry said that she had never seen a yard sale with so many things going on. "Oh," the lady said. "We always had a Spring Festival for our kids at the daycare around this time of year, so I decided to include it along with the yard sale. I am going to miss these kids so much. My husband and I are retiring and going to live in North Carolina where our kids and grandkids live, you see. I just wanted to have something nice for the parents and kids of the daycare before we left." She walked over to someone else to welcome them.

Landry found five of the little wooden picnic tables that would be perfect for the Children's Room. She also found ten wooden children's chairs. She paid for those and Adam put them in his SUV. She was shocked at the space in there after he put the third seat down. She walked over to a box and saw about twenty children's books. They looked like they were almost new and the entire box was only twenty dollars, so she got those too. Right next to those, there was a really cute sign that said "3 year old Children's Room". The signs were all separate and glued onto a rope. She figured she could remove the "3 year old" part of it and hang it on the door of the Children's Room. It was bright, primary colors. She purchased that, too.

The lady that had greeted them when they first got

there approached Landry and said, "Chloe mentioned to me that you are opening a Children's Room at the bookstore. If you are planning on movies, I have an entire box of nap mats. I can tell you that the kids at the daycare love to use them to lay on during movie time. They are brand new in the packs since I was planning to replace the ones I have. If you can use them, I would love to donate them to you."

Landry's eyes got wide. "We used those for movie time at the library I worked at in my hometown. I would love them. Please, let me pay you for them, though." She knew how nice those mats were and would be so grateful to get them for the kids.

"Oh, no. I really want to donate them. They are over here." She led Landry to a box that was away from all of the other yard sale things. Landry noticed the name of the company on the box and knew that these were top of the line. She was thrilled to get them and she thanked the woman profusely. She took the box over to Adam to put in his car. He took them, put them in the car and then walked over to a man that he knew and started talking to him.

Landry was very pleased with her purchases and decided to walk around just in case she found something else. She was smiling to herself and feeling great about all she had gotten. It had been a productive outing.

About that time, Ms. Millie walked up to her and didn't look well.

"Are you ok, Ms. Millie?" Landry looked concerned.

"I don't know. I think I must have overheated in the car earlier when I was hiding so I wouldn't get killed." Ms.

Millie was acting all pitiful.

Landry rolled her eyes. "Ms. Millie, you were not about to be killed. That truck was flying down the road in the opposite direction from us. They didn't even see us." She looked at Ms. Millie again. "But, you do look a little pekid."

She looked around and saw two of those lounge chairs that people use to lay out in the sun. They were on either side of a table and nobody was around them. She took Ms. Millie's arm and led her over there. "Here. Sit here while I go get you some water. Just lay back and relax. I am going to find you some water."

She left Ms. Millie and went to where they were selling water bottles from a bucket of ice. The lady in line in front of her was talking to the teenage girl who was running the water station. They were laughing about something and Landry awaited her turn. The lady finally left and Landry got the water. Before she turned around, she heard a very loud voice yelling.

"What are you doing, child? Personal space. Personal space. Get away from me."

Landry turned around and saw that it was Ms. Millie yelling. She took one look at her and dropped the water bottle on the ground. "OH MY LANTA." Landry said and started running over to where Ms. Millie was. She was still laying on the lounge chair but now, her entire face was painted like a bright yellow sunflower. The teenage girl that was standing beside her had a paint brush that was dripping yellow paint. Ms. Millie hauled off and swatted at the paint brush and it flew out of the girl's hand and straight into Landry's hair. She reached up without thinking and her hand smeared the yellow paint all over her red hair.

About that time Adam ran up and saw Landry's hair. "What on earth?" Then he turned toward the human sunflower that was Ms. Millie. "Oh no, oh no, oh no." He just kept repeating. "What is wrong, boy?" Ms. Millie asked. She grabbed her purse from the ground and got her compact out. She looked in the mirror and shrieked, "What did you do to me, child?!."

The young girl said, "This is where everybody sits to get their face painted for the Summer Festival. I thought you were waiting to be painted." She looked like she was going to cry at any minute.

Landry went over and patted the girl's arm. "It's ok. Just a misunderstanding. It will be alright."

"No it will not." Ms. Millie shouted. "You better hope this paint comes off of my face or I will hunt you down." The girl ran off as fast as she could and Adam helped Ms. Millie up from the chair. "Time to go, ladies."

They got in the car and Adam got out of there as fast as he could. Ms. Millie did not say a single word until they got to her house to drop her off. She got out and then looked back. "I will never go anywhere with you again, Landry. Do you understand me? Do not ask."

"Yes, ma'am. Do you want me to come in and help you get that off of your face?"

Ms. Millie just stared at her and said, "Adam. Get her outta my sight for right now or I won't be responsible for what I say." She then slammed the car door and went into her house.

Landry and Adam stopped at the bookstore to unload the things she bought. When they got to the front of Magnolia Place, he said, "Well, that went good. Nice Saturday afternoon adventure."

Landry just made a face at him and said she would see him later. She had to try to get the paint out of her hair before church tomorrow.

Chapter 17

She got in the shower and washed her hair. She saw the yellow paint going down the drain when she rinsed, so at least it was coming out. She rewashed her hair and rinsed it until there was no more yellow going down the drain. She got out and put on her robe and put her hair in a towel. At least it was washable paint so hopefully Ms. Millie wouldn't have a problem getting it off of her face.

She walked to the kitchen and started a pot of coffee. Zep was drinking some of his water and following her every move with his eyes. She needed to get started on the pies she was making to take to the farm tomorrow. She started putting the ingredients on the counter: round snack crackers, 3 egg whites, sugar, vanilla flavoring, chopped nuts, coconut. She had thawed out the whipped cream in the fridge and got that out. She got out two pie plates that she had found in Aunt Tildie's things and greased them. She made the pies and then covered them in foil and put them in the fridge to sit overnight. She got out the insulated pie carrier that she had also discovered when going through the items in the apartment. She would put the pies in before she left for Church tomorrow. It would keep them fresh until she got to the farm. She put the dishes in the dishwasher and cleaned up her mess just as her phone rang.

She picked up. "Hi, Miss Burke. This is Brad Larson, James Larson's son."

"Hi, Brad. How has your father been doing since we

last spoke?"

"Actually, he is doing fantastic. Everyone has been so surprised at how well he is healing, especially at his age. They are telling us that he will be able to go to rehab next week and will be there for a couple of weeks and then hopefully will come home but will have to have someone stay with him at least part time. His Physical Therapist and Occupational Therapist will come to his apartment two or three times a week so that he doesn't have to go out. I just have to find someone who is willing to sit with him while he is awake and moving about during the day until he is fully recovered. I have tried to convince him to come to Michigan with me so that my wife can take care of him. My kids would love having him there, too. He refuses and says he wants to be at his 'home' and where he is comfortable. I understand that but you would think he would at least consider coming to stay with us. We have plenty of room and even have a bedroom on the first floor of our home for him." Landry could hear him sigh.

"I wish he would come with family at least until he heals so that the worry could be taken away on your part." Landry commented. "I may have a solution for you, though. Let me speak with someone I know and see if we can work out a way that he can stay in his apartment and still comply with his needs. I will get back with you soon." Landry hung up. She would work on that problem later.

Something was nagging her about these crimes. There was something that Landry felt was important that she had heard but she couldn't remember what it was or who she heard it from. "Oh, well." she thought. "Hopefully it will come to me." She decided to take Zep for a walk before they settled in for the night. She had pulled her hair up in a ponytail and had put on some jeans and a t-shirt, so all she had to do was get on her ankle boots.

She and Zep walked into the lobby and Orvis was just hanging up the phone. "Oh, Miss Burke. I was just getting ready to buzz you. Maisy from over at the bookstore said her Mom is on the way to pick her up for the day. She wants to know if she can come over and speak to you before she goes home?"

"Of course. Please let her know that I will be in the conference room waiting for her." Landry had an idea of what Maisy may want to talk about and she didn't want to discuss it in front of anyone. She and Zep waited in the conference room and suddenly the door opened. "Hey, Boss Lady." Maisy said and closed the door behind her. She picked Zep up and hugged him. She held him in her lap and said, "I wanted to let you know that I talked to Jenna and she has agreed to go to the Church and look through the Secret Closet for a dress. She was reluctant until I explained what you said about the dresses not being from anyone here locally. I told her to go Monday after Ms. Millie left for the day and said that I would work by myself until she got back. I hope that is alright."

"That's perfect, Maisy.," Landry said. "I am just so happy that she has agreed but I wonder if the boy who asked her has found someone else to take since Jenna told him she couldn't go."

"Nope. As soon as she agreed to find a dress at the Church, she called him to see if he still wanted to take her. He said that of course he did and she told him she accepted his invitation. I am praying that this has a happy ending. Jenna deserves to have some fun. She doesn't seem to have many friends."

"I hope it works out perfectly, Maisy. I hope she knows that she has a friend in you." Landry smiled and patted Maisy's arm.

"Well, I gotta run. My Mom's outside in the car and I have a paper that I need to work on for school. See ya later, Boss Lady." Maisy got up, handed Zep back to Landry and rushed out of the door.

Landry and Zep went on their walk and, thankfully, didn't run into any cats. When they got back, Landry noticed that it was 6:45pm. She stopped and asked Orvis if any of the Pink Hat Ladies group had arrived for the event they had scheduled. He told her that Mrs. Cartwright had just come in and that the caterers had arrived around 6. About that time, three women walked in the lobby door. They all had some variation of a pink hat on and were dressed to the nines. They smiled at Landry and Orvis and went to the elevator. "Orvis, thank you for staying tonight until all of them are gone and the event room is locked. If you have any problems or concerns, give me a call." Landry waited until she saw that the women had gotten to the fifth floor before she and Zep went up.

Her phone rang as soon as she walked in the door to her apartment. "Hey, Landry." It was Adam. "Any chance

Wyatt and I can stop by for just a minute? He said he has something to talk to us about regarding the investigation."

"Sure, that's fine. I will put on some coffee and we can finish off that apple pie Wyatt brought over here."

"Great. I will let him know and we will stop by shortly." Adam hung up.

Wyatt was the first to arrive. "Thanks for seeing me, Landry. I have some things I need to talk over with you and Adam. This case is making me lose my mind. Is that fresh coffee I smell?"

"Yep. Sit down, Wyatt. I will get you a cup." Just as she turned to go to the kitchen, there was a knock on the door. She changed direction and let Adam in and told him to have a seat and that she would bring him a coffee when she got hers and Wyatt's.

The guys talked while she got the coffee ready and plated a piece of apple pie for each of them. After they were all seated and Zep had gotten his petting from both of them, Wyatt began. "I put a question in the private group on the internet that we have for Sheriff's. We share information about unsolved crimes in case other areas have similar crimes happening and have information that will be helpful to each other. It seems that other small towns are experiencing art thefts at higher rates than ever before. We all got on a conference call and this is what we think is happening. Thieves are targeting small towns where they know there are some very valuable paintings. They are stealing them and selling them on the black market. An underground art black market. We think they are going to small towns because that is usually where security is lacking and then can easily break in and get what they are looking for. For instance, a small town in Alabama had one of its historical houses broken into and two very valuable paintings were stolen. The house is out in the country and tourists come to visit and see the historical site and artifacts, including paintings, that are in the house. The reason we think it is an art theft ring is that there were other valuable items on display there but only the paintings were stolen. There was a security system in place but it was an older version and was pretty easy to disarm."

He ate some of his pie and sipped some coffee, then continued. "Another small town in South Dakota had a little museum broken into six months ago. The Sheriff there said that looking at the outside of that place, you would think it was just an old building with nothing of value in it. But, a famous artist donated some paintings he did of Mount Rushmore and The Crazy Horse Memorial to the museum because he was born and raised in that small town. Also, six different Sheriffs said that houses of people in their towns had been broken into while nobody was at home. In every case, the houses were owned by people of 'old money' that liked to collect art and display it in their home.

"Wow" Adam put down his fork and said. "Have there been anymore murders related to these art thefts or did those just happen here in Bobwhite Mountain?"

Wyatt shook his head. He had finished the pie and was drinking the rest of his coffee. "So far, we are the only town that has had murders occur around the same time as the art thefts. It is baffling all the way around. The main reason I wanted to talk to you tonight, Landry, is that during one of my quiet times that I sit and try to figure out a mess like this, I thought about Glenn Mayhew that lives on this floor. I know you said he works for a security company and that they are going to install cameras here for you in the building. What do you know about this guy?"

Landry looked surprised. She had eaten her pie while Wyatt was filling them in. "Not much. Just what Lisa told me when I first came to town and she was filling me in on the residents in the building. He seems like a nice person. He was very prompt with getting me the information on the cameras from his company. They are supposed to come next week to start installing everything. From what he told me, he is a salesman for them; he goes out and talks to businesses and homeowners who want security installed. He then gives the information to someone else in the company and they get everything ready for the actual installers. Do you think he is guilty of these crimes?" She sounded alarmed.

Wyatt thought for a second and said, "I'm not sure. I mean, he could probably disarm the security devices but from what Lisa told me, he is out of town a lot since he works this entire side of the state. She called it his district and it encompasses a large area from what he has told her."

"Also," Wyatt continued, "My deputies didn't ever catch up with the old truck. Whoever was driving it probably went down some back roads and into the deep woods. I have told every law enforcement agency around to be on the lookout. I have a sneaky feeling that truck is involved in more ways than one in all of this."

"Thanks for letting us know all of this, Wyatt." Adam looked at Landry. "I know he is probably not involved in this but it makes me very nervous that Mayhew lives right down the hall from you. He could even be the one to have left those notes. Do you want me to stay in the den until all this is over? I get up very early to get to work so we probably wouldn't even have to see each other in the mornings."

Wyatt spoke up, "I think that is an excellent idea, Landry. At least he would be close by if something happened."

"No!" Landry shouted. "I am not a helpless child. I will be fine here by myself. I have a whole building full of people around me."

Very calmly Adam replied, "But they are all on other floors, Landry. Mayhew and you are the only ones on this floor. I am not saying he is a bad guy...in fact, I am praying he isn't. I just don't feel comfortable with you being here by yourself with him right down the hall, that's all."

Landry sighed and replied just as calmly, "I know and I appreciate both of you worrying about me. But, I will be fine. Go home. I have to get some rest before Church and the farm tomorrow. Go...get out. Both of you."

"Well, I guess she told us." Wyatt laughed. "I will catch up with y'all later." He got up and gave Zep one last pet and went home.

Adam did the same thing after he gave Landry a solemn look and shook his head at her. "I will pick you up tomorrow. Just be careful, Landry."

Chapter 18

The next morning, Landry got up and took Zep for a walk. When they got back, she had a couple of waffles with the leftover strawberries in her refrigerator and Zep ate his food and ran from room to room like he was practicing for a car race. He loved to run as fast as he could, stop on a dime and then run just as fast in the opposite direction. She got dressed for church in a short sleeved mint green dress and put a matching ribbon in her hair to try to control it a little. She got the pies out of the refrigerator and put them in the pie carrier and zipped it up. After she got Zep settled in the den, she grabbed her purse and the pie carrier and went down to the lobby to wait on Adam.

She wasn't there five minutes when he pulled up. She saw that his Mom, Judith, was in the front seat. Adam's sister, Ivy was in the back and Landry climbed in next to her and introduced herself as she put the pie carrier in the floorboard between her feet. "I am so glad to meet you, Ivy. It sounds like you have a pretty exciting job that takes you to lots of different places."

"I am glad to meet you, too, Landry. And, yes, I love my job. Until I decide to settle down and have a family, I want to travel as much as I can. This is the perfect job for that." Ivy smiled at her.

When they got to the Church, Landry went to the backdoor since it was her turn to teach Children's Church this week. She loved doing it and the time flew by. They were on the way to the farm before she knew it. As they pulled up, Landry got a funny feeling in her chest. She had spent so many happy times here as a child. She always felt safe and content at the farm.

She took in the big, white house with the wrap around porch. She could still see Aunt Tildie sitting in a porch rocker shelling beans while she sang, "In The Garden". That was her favorite hymn and she sang it often. Landry could tell that the house had been painted and the porch furniture had been replaced with new items, but the feel of the farmhouse was the same. The large concrete blocks on each side of the steps had potted plants on them that were blooming and beautiful.

As she walked up the steps, the third one creaked just as it had when she was younger. She went up on the porch and placed her hand on the outside wall of the house. It was as if she could feel Aunt Tildie's presence. She turned around and looked out over the land. It was almost like a dream but at the same time, it was just as she remembered. She got tears in her eyes and just stood there staring for a while. When she wiped her eyes, she noticed that the others had stood back at the car and let her reminisce and take it all in by herself. She waved them up to the porch.

They went into the house and Adam introduced her to his Aunt and Uncle. They said that they felt like they already knew her since Lisa talked about her so much. Steve and Denise Wilcox were warm and welcoming to Landry and when she told Denise that she had brought pies, Denise thought that was so sweet and took them into the kitchen. Landry followed her and saw that it had been remodeled since the Wilcox's had bought the farm.

Denise offered to take Landry on a tour of the house and Landry happily accepted. As she walked the halls and saw the rooms, Landry was happy to see that most of them remained the same except for some new paint and flooring. The layout was basically as it always had been. She touched everything and even recognized some of the furniture in the study that Aunt Tildie had left when she moved to Magnolia Place. Landry was in a daze. She knew that this was no longer Aunt Tildie's home, but yet it felt the same to her. Denise touched her arm and when Landry turned to her, Denise was holding something out to her.

Landry lost it then. Her emotions were all over the place and when she saw what Denise was holding, she burst into tears. It was the quilt that Aunt Tildie and Landry had made during the last summer that Landry came to Bobwhite Mountain when she was young. The material was rabbits and flowers and Aunt Tildie had let Landry pick it out. They worked that entire summer on the quilt. When she left to go back home, Aunt Tildie kept the quilt so that she could put the border on it. She had told Landry later that the quilt was finished and that she would mail it to her. Landry asked her not to do that and to keep it at the farm where they made it. She had regretted that decision the day she heard of Aunt Tildie's death. She wished she had the quilt to remember that last summer.

Denise was handing the quilt to her. She said, "Landry, when Tildie was removing the things from the house that she wanted to take with her, she personally gave me this quilt and told me that you had said to leave it at the farm where it was made. Now that Tildie is gone, I feel that you should have it. She told me how the two of you made it and it was such a wonderful memory to her."

Landry smiled through her tears and took the quilt. "Thank you so much, Denise. You have no idea what this means to me." Landry took it to the living room and put it on top of her purse to take back home with her and joined the others as they talked and laughed.

After a while, Lisa came in and spoke to everyone and gave hugs. She turned to Landry, "I am so glad you came today. It seems strange seeing you away from work, though." She laughed.

Landry noticed a picture on the mantle of a man in a Navy uniform. She asked Lisa about him. "Oh, that's my older brother, Parker. You remember Adam and me telling you about him from when we were younger, right? He's in the Navy and stationed in the Philippines right now. I miss him being here at the farm for all the family to get together, but he really loves being in the service." She took Landry's arm and led her to the kitchen as Denise announced that dinner was ready. They all took their seats and Steve said the blessing.

After dinner they sat around the table to talk and laugh. Then, Denise brought in the dessert and coffee. She had made a coconut cake and some cookies. She also brought the pies that Landry had made. Everyone said how wonderful the pies looked and asked what kind they were.

Landry proudly said, "It is a favorite in my family. We make them for every holiday. They are Possum Pies". It got very quiet and a few of the guests reached for the coconut cake.

"Uh, possum pies?" Adam asked. "I, uh, don't think I have ever had those. Where in the world did you get possum from, Landry?" It hit Landry at that moment that she needed to explain and fast. She laughed and said, "Oh, no. They don't have possum in them. That is just the name of them. You know how a possum plays dead when a predator comes near? It causes the possum to go into shock and into a comatose state that can last anywhere from 40 minutes to several hours. Anyway, the story goes that this pie is named that because it 'plays possum' and represents itself as something else. The ingredients that are included are not the normal ones you would expect. But all of them are delicious in their own right and when combined, the flavor is wonderful. They all looked at each other and burst out laughing. They got a piece of the pie and said that it was delicious. "I have to get the recipe from you, Landry." Judith said. "This would be a great conversation starter for my guests at the B&B."

Landry reached in her purse and got out a tiny recorder that was in there. "Possum Pie recipe to Judith." She spoke into the recorder and put it back in her purse. At everyone's questioning looks, she said "With everything I have to remember between the bookstore and the apartment building, along with trying to keep up with the names of all the new people I am meeting here in Bobwhite Mountain, I decided to get this handy little machine. At the end of each day, I play back what I have recorded during the day and make lists or notes of what I need to do."

"Pretty smart." Ivy replied. "Our doctors at the hospital do that and then record their doctor's orders and notes for us to put in the patient charts on another recorder for a transcriptionist to type. That way, they have the first recorder to rewind and check information if they need to."

After they were done with dessert, they all pitched in to do the dishes. While they were doing that, Landry looked at Lisa and said, "I have never asked you. Where do you live, Lisa?"

Lisa answered, "Oh, I live in Mom and Dad's old house. The one I grew up in."

"Yep." said Steve. "The house is paid for so when we decided to buy this place, we offered it to Lisa so that she would only have to pay for utilities. She is trying to save up to build her own house here on the farm. And, having a roommate, she only has to pay half of the utilities so that helps with saving money."

"Who is your roommate, Lisa? Anyone I know?" Landry asked her. "Probably. You know the teller at the bank, Hannah Torres?"

"I sure do. She is such a nice person. I have never seen her without a smile on her face. She is your roommate?"

"She is. And, you are right. She is the perfect roommate to have. Never had any problems and we get along great. She dates Dave Lemke." Lisa said.

"Lemke...that name sounds familiar to me." Landry

had a curious look on her face.

"He is the son of Barry Lemke, the owner of Barry's Hardware in town." Lisa told her.

Landry snapped her fingers and said, "That's it. I am trying to remember everybody's name and sometimes my mind just gets overloaded."

Then, Adam asked Landry to walk around the farm with him. She was taking in all the changes as well as the things she remembered about the farm when Adam stopped. She looked up and there was a beautiful Magnolia tree in front of her. "Oh, Adam. It is so gorgeous."

Adam said, "Your Aunt Tildie planted it years ago. She said it was a sprig off of the one in front of the library in Bent Branch. Landry, there is something else. You see this area in front of it with the concrete border and white gravel?" Landry looked at the ground and replied, "Yes. Those flowers in the container are so pretty. They look like jasmine."

Adam replied, "They are. Landry this is where I put Miss Tildie's ashes. She wanted to be on the farm and I thought there was no other place that was right except under her favorite tree."

"Oh, Adam." Landry whispered with tears streaming down her face. "It is absolutely perfect. Thank you so much for loving my Aunt and doing this for her." Her throat was tight and she was overcome with emotion.

Adam put his arm around her and said, "That's what friends do. We take care of each other even after death. She was so good to me in every way and I miss her so much."

They stood there for a while, composed themselves and then turned to go back to the house. At that moment, Adam's phone rang. "Hey, Wyatt," he said when he answered. "What's up?" Adam listened for a minute and said, "Sure. We are on our way." He then told Landry that they had to go to the Sheriff's Department right away.

They told everyone goodbye and Adam's Mom and sister said that they would get Lisa to drive them back to the B&B when she left. Landry and Adam got in his car. Landry got her purse and the quilt before leaving.

"What is it, Adam? Is something wrong?" Landry asked once they were in Adam's car.

"Wyatt said that his deputies finally found the truck. It was over in Wrigley Springs and got into a high speed chase with the cops over there. The occupants were Scat and his brother, Lee. Wyatt has them in separate interrogation rooms and wants us to come take a look at them. He said he would explain more when we got there." Landry answered, "Ok. You know, Adam, I still have a feeling that I heard something from someone that may be important. I just cannot for the life of me remember what it was or who I heard it from. It is driving me crazy." She turned toward the window and tried to think real hard about it but couldn't remember.

When they got to Wyatt inside the Sheriff's Department, he took them to the hallway in front of the interrogation rooms. "Ok. First, Adam, look at the man in this room and tell me if he was one of the people you saw in the truck with Fred on separate occasions." Scat was seated in the room.

Adam looked in and said, "Yep. No doubt about it. He is the one I saw with Fred the first time. I was behind them and this guy kept turning around to look at something behind the seat in the truck."

"Great. Now, Landry. We are going down to this other room and I want you to look in and see if you recognize the guy from anywhere."

Landry walked up to the one way window and looked in. The man was standing with his back to her. She stared at him for a minute and turned to Wyatt. "That is the man I saw running from Fred's trailer before I found Melodie's body."

Wyatt nodded his head. "We have taken his DNA and my lab is working to compare it to the DNA we collected from under Melodie's fingernails."

"Who is this guy?" Landry asked Wyatt.

Wyatt told her, "He is Lee Garrison. Scat's brother. Lee is the one that was driving the truck when the deputies caught them. They brought both of them in for eluding police and I noticed the long blonde hair on Lee. I had a hunch he was the guy you saw at the trailer." Wyatt turned around at the sound of his name. It was one of his deputies.

"Sir, the lab just got back in touch. The DNA is a match. We finally know who killed Melodie and he is in that room." He pointed to Lee.

Landry started shaking and sweating profusely. She was twisting her ring and was very dizzy. Adam grabbed her and sat her on the bench that was in the hallway. Wyatt looked at Adam and nodded in the direction of the room Lee was in. Adam told him he understood that work was calling and he would sit with Landry. He got on his knees in front of her and told her to do her breathing exercises. He could tell this was a very bad panic attack.

She was shaking so bad her teeth chattered but she started breathing in through her nose and out through her mouth. Adam stayed right with her and let her work on it herself. When she finally got herself under control, she had tears streaming down her face and she looked Adam in the eyes.

"He slashed Melodie's throat, Adam. He killed her. I was on the porch when he came out of that trailer. I was right there. He could have easily killed me, too. And, Ms. Millie was in the car. What if…" she trailed off.

Adam looked her straight in the eyes and put his hands on her shoulders to steady her. "Landry, listen to me. You know and I know that the Lord watches over us. My Mom always said that He watches over children and fools, along with everyone else. You might have been a fool that day for going there but He kept you safe. He has plans for you, Landry. Now, you are not on that porch. You are here with me and you are safe. Try to calm down if you can. I am going to get you some water." he smiled at her.

When Adam came back with the water, Wyatt approached and looked at Landry. "You ok? I'm sorry I had to walk away but my deputies had some questions that I had to answer. I know this has to be very traumatizing, Landry. She answered him, "I am alright. It did all hit me at once but I am calm now. Thanks for asking, Wyatt."

"Uh, Wyatt.," Adam spoke up. "I know I said that the person I had seen with Fred in the truck the other time looked like a female but, this guy in here with the long blonde hair is very tall and thin. It could have been him in the truck. He had that hoodie on at the time, but I really think it could be the same person."

Wyatt turned around without saying a word. He walked into his office and came out with a dark colored hoodie. "Stand right there, Adam."

He walked into the interrogation room and handed the hoodie to Lee. They could see that he was arguing that he didn't want to put the hoodie on. Wyatt said something to him and Lee made a mean face but put it on and sat back down in the chair. Wyatt told him to put the hood up. Lee shook his head no and Wyatt walked over and yanked the hood on his head. Landry heard Adam whisper, "That's him."

Wyatt came back out with the hoodie and threw it in the trash. "It's my old one that I keep here but I don't want to touch it again. Adam?," he questioned.

Adam answered, "It's him, Wyatt. I am one hundred percent positive. His hair was sticking out of your hoodie just like on the day I saw him with Fred." Wyatt nodded and told them they could leave.

Chapter 19

Because she had so much happen that day, Landry was mentally and physically exhausted and went right to sleep when she got home. She woke up the next morning to find Zep licking her face. She laughed and got dressed to take him for a short walk. When they got back to Magnolia Place, Lisa was there. "Morning Landry. Morning Zep." she said. "Where did you and Adam have to rush off to yesterday?"

Landry took her into the conference room, swore her to secrecy and explained to her what happened at the Sheriff's Department. Lisa asked if Lee was also responsible for Fred's murder. "Unfortunately, no. They still don't have a lead on that. It was a different DNA that they collected from his crime scene." She turned to go back upstairs when Lisa exclaimed, "Oh, Landry. I forgot to tell you that Mr. Mayhew called right before you came in. He said that his company installers should be here Friday to put the cameras in. I reminded him about the two you want for Jasmine Bloom and he said they would do those at the same time."

Landry thanked Lisa and went back to her apartment. She was glad they were getting the cameras but she couldn't forget the concerns that Wyatt and Adam had about Mr. Mayhew. She hoped they were totally wrong about him.

When she got back to her apartment, she decided to

make Ms. Millie a quiche and take it to the bookstore as a peace offering. She turned on some music and gave Zep a few of his treats. She had a frozen deep dish pie shell in the freezer. She took it out and punched some holes in the bottom crust with a fork and set it aside. Then, she cracked six eggs in a bowl and beat them up. To that, she added some finely diced fresh mushrooms, spinach, chopped black olives and shredded cheese. She also added a little milk, salt and pepper. She mixed it all together in the bowl and poured it into the pie shell. She put it in the oven at 350. It should be ready in about 30 minutes, or whenever the eggs set.

While she was waiting for it to get done, she called Lisa and asked her if she knew if Ms. Goode that lived on the 3rd floor was in today. Landry knew that she was a Home Care Provider and might be out working. Lisa said, "She sure is. She and her daughter, Penney, just got back from shopping. They went out early this morning. You know, Penney will graduate this year and is going on a cruise. She wanted to pick up some new clothes for that as well as her Prom dress. Ms. Goode is off today and Penney only goes to school in the afternoon since she already has all the credits she needs to graduate."

"Perfect." Landry replied. "Could you call her and make sure it is ok for me to drop by in about 30 minutes? I have something I need to talk to her about."

Lisa called Landry back in just a minute. "Ms. Goode said that it would be fine for you to stop by. She is not planning to go out anymore today."

Landry got out her recipe box and wrote down the recipe for the Possum Pie. She would go by the B&B later and drop off the recipe to Judith. The oven timer dinged and she checked to be sure the quiche was done. It was and she took it out and covered it in foil. She left it on the top of the warm stove until she came back to get it after talking to Ms. Goode.

When she got to Ms. Goode's apartment, Penney let her in and then left saying that she was going for a jog before she came back to shower and get ready for her afternoon classes at the high school. Ms. Goode greeted Landry with a smile and invited her to sit down and asked what she could do for her.

Landry told Ms. Goode about Mr. Larson's situation. "I know you probably have all of the patients you can handle but, just in case, I thought I would ask you about taking him on since you are a private caregiver. His apartment is only one floor down and he knows you which might make it easier on him to accept the help from you."

Ms. Goode broke out in a huge smile. "Mr. Larson is a card. He has grilled out with Penney and me several times. He has even picked Penney up from school when my car was broken. Of course, that was a few years ago when he was more able to drive. I knew him and his wife when they ran the Feed and Seed store here in town. His wife was a wonderful woman and I was glad when he decided to move here in town after she passed away. He had told us that he had gotten so lonely after she was gone."

Ms. Goode asked Landry if she would like some sweet

tea and went into the kitchen to make it for both of them. When she sat back down, she said, "You won't believe this but I have actually been a little worried. You see, one of my patients left the area last week to go live with her daughter. Then on Friday I found out that another patient, who had to go to the hospital in the middle of the night early last week, had sadly passed away. That leaves me with just two patients. One only needs me a few hours a couple of days a week since his wife can handle his care the other days. The other one needs me to sit with her every night. She has Sundowner's and her sister, who is usually her caregiver, works at night. She is off on Mondays and Tuesdays, but all of the other nights I stay with her since she can't be there alone. So, if Mr. Larson would be alright to stay alone at night a couple of nights a week and for a few hours a couple of days a week, I would love to take him on as a patient. Hopefully, he will do good and be back to his old self soon."

"That is the plan. His son, Brad, said that PT and OT will come to his apartment to work with him. He will probably need help with basic activities of daily living in the beginning until he can walk again. Also, running errands like picking up his medicine, groceries and such. Is that doable for you?"

"It sure is." Ms. Goode replied.

"Alright. I haven't even proposed this to Brad yet, so let me do that. If you are ok with it, I will pass along your number and the two of you can work out the details. I know that Mr. Larson will be going to rehab for two weeks before he comes home." Ms. Goode agreed and Landry thanked her and said goodbye.

She then left and went back to her own apartment to pick up the quiche and her purse. Zep was sleeping after his walk this morning and eating all of the treats she had given him. She left to go to the bookstore.

She walked in and saw Ms. Millie at one of the shelves rearranging books. She took a deep breath and said, "Good morning, Ms. Millie. I hope your day is going well." She heard Ms. Millie reply under her breath and it sounded like she said, "It was."

Landry cleared her throat and said, "I am sorry, Ms. Millie. I had no idea that girl would paint your face when I told you to sit there. I know you're mad at me but it really wasn't my fault. I would have been glad to help you wash it off. I offered, you know."

"Child, I know it wasn't your fault. I am just trying to keep my distance from you before I get hurt real bad. I have had more bad things happen to me lately than I have in my whole life."

"Well, I am sorry that you feel like I am a jinx where you are concerned. I don't mean to be. Also, I made you a quiche. I thought we might sit together and have some. Could we do that at least?" Landry asked her.

Ms. Millie thought for a minute. "I guess so. I forgive you, Landry. Just please try to not put me in those situations anymore."

Landry smiled. "I will try my very best. Now, let's go eat before the quiche gets cold or customers come in."

They went to the office and Landry poured them some coffee while Ms. Millie got a plastic knife and a couple of plates. They sat down and Ms. Millie said the blessing. She looked at the quiche and said, "Are those black olives?"

"Yes," said Landry. "I hope you like black olives."

"Oh, yes. I love them. What I don't like is the green olives. Tildie loved those but they are just too salty for me. The black ones are just right." She said as she took a bite.

Landry agreed. "I don't care for the green ones, either. I do like kalamata olives, though. Those are a good 'in between' olive. Not too salty and not too bland."

Ms. Millie nodded and took another bite of the quiche. She said, "This is so good. You got your cooking skills from your Aunt. That woman could cook anything and make it taste like heaven."

Landry ate another bite and said, "She is the one who taught me how to make this. She said there was a more complicated way but, to her, this one tasted just as go…" She looked up at the moment and saw the biggest eyes she had ever seen. Ms. Millie's eyes were huge and she was clutching her throat.

"What is it?" Landry screamed. She jumped up and started hitting Ms. Millie in the back thinking she was choking. Ms. Millie was shaking her head back and forth and finally got out the words, "mushrooms".

Landry said, "Are you choking on a mushroom? But, I diced them up really small. They shouldn't be big enough to choke you."

Ms. Millie was still shaking her head and forced out

"allergic" and grabbed her stomach and moaned before she fell out of the chair.

"Oh no! Ms. Millie please don't die on me. I love you, I promise." She grabbed the phone and called 911 then she sat on the floor with Ms. Millie's head in her lap until the ambulance got there. Ms. Millie kept clutching her stomach and saying something that sounded like 'jinx' but Landry couldn't really be sure since Ms. Millie's tongue and mouth were swollen so bad. She was so happy when the EMT's walked in.

Landry was sitting in the ER waiting room when she saw Adam walking up. "Hey," he said. "I thought that was you. What's wrong?"

"What are you doing here?" Landry asked him. She felt like she was in the twilight zone and she couldn't think.

"I asked you first, but I was giving a class that the hospital sponsors on Wills, Living Wills and Estates. Now, why are you here?" Adam said.

"I tried to kill Ms. Millie."

"Landry, don't joke about something like that." Adam looked surprised.

"Not joking. See, I made her a quiche and took it to the bookstore as a peace offering after the whole face painting debacle. We were in the office eating some of it when she started grabbing her throat. Seems she is highly allergic to mushrooms which I put in the quiche. I called 911 and they came and popped an epi-pen into her thigh and brought her here to have her stomach pumped." She had tears in her eyes. "Adam, I know you told me that I wasn't but, I truly think I am a jinx. At least where Ms. Millie is concerned. She probably won't even want to be near me again. She might even quit the bookstore."

Adam looked at her. "Landry, there was no way you could have known she was allergic to mushrooms. It was an accident. You got her help and she is going to be alright. You are not a jinx."

Right then, a doctor walked up to the nurses desk and asked a question. The nurse pointed at Landry and he walked over. "Miss Burke? I am Dr. Joseph. Ms. Wells is going to be fine. She is in a room now and we will keep her overnight.

"Oh, thank you so much. I am so happy that she is alright. Can I go see her now?" Landry asked and reached for her purse. Dr. Joseph paused. "Uh…Miss Burke. Actually, Ms. Wells has asked that you not be allowed in her room. I'm sorry."

Landry looked at Adam. "I told you. Let's go." They got up to leave and the doctor looked at Adam. "Mr. Wilcox, Ms. Wells asked me to tell you that she needed an appointment with you at your office at your earliest convenience." Landry's eyes got big. "What? She's going to sue me? I had no idea she was allergic to mushrooms. She can't do that, can she Adam?"

Adam started to speak but the doctor interrupted. "No, no. Nothing like that. She said she wants to get her Will in order before she sees you again." He looked at Landry.

"Perfect. Just perfect." Landry got up and walked out.

Chapter 20

After Landry went back to the bookstore and threw away the rest of the quiche, she sat down at the front desk to stay until Jenna and Maisy got there. She just could not believe what had happened. She called Lisa at Magnolia Place and explained it all to her and then told her that she would be at the bookstore until 3:30. When she hung up, she walked to the Children's Room. Chloe had completed the murals and they were breathtaking. She loved them. Just then, she heard the bell ring over the front door as it opened and two guys walked in with a roll of carpet.

"Perfect timing." she told them and showed them to the room. The carpet store had a website so she had picked out what she wanted and called to tell them. They told her they would be here Monday or Tuesday to install it. They were very prompt, she thought.

When she thought about their website, she pulled up the one for Jasmine Bloom Books. It was sort of blah…just the basic stuff. She took her little recorder out and said, "Ask Zack about the website." She knew he was a computer programmer and she would ask him if he would like to update the bookstore website during his shifts at Magnolia Place.

As she clicked "close" on the computer, two customers came in. After that, it was a steady stream of customers until Jenna and Maisy showed up. Landry filled them in on the happenings that morning. She just told them that Ms.

Millie wasn't feeling well, so she took her shift. If Ms. Millie wanted to tell them that she had tried to kill her, she could. Landry wasn't saying a word.

When she left Jasmine Bloom, she went to Magnolia Place. She ran up to check on Zep and give him fresh water and food. Then, she got her car from the garage and headed to Judith's B&B. When she got there, Judith was in a rocking chair on the front porch.

"Hey, Landry. What a nice surprise. I just made some fresh lemonade. Would you like a glass of that and a sandwich?" Judith asked.

"I would. I haven't eaten all day and I am so hungry." Landry replied. She decided that the couple of bites of quiche didn't count since she wasn't mentioning it to anyone.

Judith got up and went inside to get the food. Landry sat down in one of the rockers and looked around at all of the gorgeous flowers that were starting to bloom. Aunt Tildie loved flowers so much. Judith's were varied in color and she could tell that when they all bloomed, it was going to be beautiful. The yard reminded her of an English garden. So bright and pretty.

Judith came back out and put the tray on the small table between them. "Here is your lemonade and a ham sandwich. I cooked ham last night for the guests' dinner tonight. I put a little mayonnaise and tomato on it for you and put some chips on the side. Eat up."

Landry ate and sipped her lemonade. She and Judith talked about flowers and then Landry remembered why she had come by. "Here is the Possum Pie recipe that you wanted." She handed it to Judith.

Judith thanked her and Landry told her that she had to get home now and check with Lisa before she left for the day. She left as Judith stood on the porch waving her off and smiling.

When she got back to Magnolia Place, Landry stopped at Lisa's desk and asked her to please leave a note for Zack and ask him about updating the website. She then went upstairs and called the hospital to check on Ms. Millie. The nurse at the desk said that Ms. Millie was fine and would be coming home tomorrow. Ms. Millie had also left a message saying that should Miss Burke call, to let her know that Mr. Wilcox would be taking her home from the hospital. Landry thanked the nurse and hung up. She put Zep's leash on and took him for a walk, again avoiding the park for the time being. When they got back home, her phone rang. It was Wyatt and he said he was with Adam and they wanted to know if they could stop by. "Of course. I am in for the night. I thought about ordering pizza tonight. If that is good with y'all, what toppings do you want?"

She could hear them speaking to each other and Wyatt came back on the line and said, "We both just want pepperoni, cheese and green peppers. We will be there shortly. Thanks Landry."

She ordered two large pizzas. She went to the kitchen to see if she had anything for dessert. Then, she remembered buying ice cream at the grocery store and decided that would do. She then went and freshened up and put on her comfortable sweatpants and a t-shirt. There was a knock on the door and it was Wyatt and Adam.

Wyatt told them that Lee had talked to them with his lawyer present and had confessed to Melodie's murder after they told him they had his DNA at the scene. He swore he did not have anything to do with Fred's murder, which they knew because his DNA was nowhere at that crime scene and the one they had belonged to a female. He wouldn't say why he was seen in the truck with Fred and he clammed up after that and said he wouldn't implicate anyone else even if he knew anything, which he claimed not to. He was being held for murder. They still had Fred's unsolved murder and the thefts to deal with. Scat also would not tell them why he was in the truck with Fred when Adam saw him. Scat couldn't make bond and was being held until his trial on the eluding police and endangerment charges.

"By the way, they both denied having anything to do with a note being put under a door." Wyatt said.

The pizza arrived and they ate it while Adam and Landry informed Wyatt of the day's activities involving Ms. Millie. Wyatt almost choked on his soda when Landry told them about Ms. Millie asking Adam to bring her home tomorrow. "Man, Landry. You might want to find somebody else to pick on. Ms. Millie can get petty about stuff. You want to stay on her good side." Wyatt laughed.

"I am afraid that ship has sailed, Wyatt. She thinks I am trying to get her killed. I have no idea how to make her see that nothing is farther from the truth. I love that woman."

Landry went into the kitchen and got the ice cream out. She told the guys to come pick the kind they wanted. She had toppings to choose from…chocolate syrup, caramel syrup, strawberries, nuts and a bottle of maraschino cherries. She also had some whipped cream leftover in the fridge. They all made their ice cream sundaes and went out on the balcony to eat them. Adam grabbed two of Zep's treats and gave them to him since he had followed the group outside. They talked about all sorts of things and marveled at the lights on the mountain. Wyatt joked to Adam that his townhome was probably one of the houses they were seeing. Adam refuted that since he said he didn't leave any lights on at his house while he was gone. They all yawned at the same time and went back to the living room.

Wyatt and Adam left about 20 minutes later. Landry was tired and decided that she wanted to take a shower and read. Zep got in the bed with her and he snored while she read the rest of a book that she was interested in.

The next few days went by in a blur. Landry worked at the bookstore so that Ms. Millie could rest and get her strength back up, although Landry had an ulterior motive. She was hoping that with a little time Ms. Millie would forgive her.. Zack had agreed to update the website for both Jasmine Bloom Books and Magnolia Place and said that he would come in an hour early tonight to get her input. Landry went down to the lobby when he came in early at 7pm and they talked about what she wanted to do with the separate websites. He sounded more confident than her and was definitely way more experienced with computers. She left it to him after she wrote down a few notes. She was still sitting there when the elevator dinged and Penney Goode and her Mom got out. Penney was like a fairy princess. She had on a pink prom dress that was floor length and glittery. It was a one-shoulder dress and fit Penney perfectly. She had on coordinating shoes. At that moment, her date knocked on the lobby door. Landry opened it for him and he had a beautiful wrist corsage in a box in his hand.

"This is my date, Ian Davis, everyone." Penney said. As everyone said hello to him, he put the corsage on Penney's wrist and Mary Goode took lots of pictures of her daughter and date in the lobby.

"I thought prom was always held on Friday night." Zack questioned.

"Normally it is but, tomorrow is a school holiday so they are doing it tonight." Penney answered. She then kissed her Mom goodbye and she and Ian left. Landry suddenly wondered if Jenna and her date had gotten off to prom yet. She sure wished that she could see Jenna in the dress she chose.

Mary and Landry got on the elevator at the same time to go up. Mary said to Landry, "I wanted to let you know that Brad Larson has already gotten in touch. We are making arrangements for Mr. Larson to come here to his apartment after rehab. His son sounds like a very nice man."

"Wonderful, Ms. Goode. I was hoping it would work out."

"Miss Burke, please call me Mary. Everybody does,

even my patients." Mary smiled. They reached the third floor and Landry said, "Only if you call me Landry." They both nodded and Landry went up to the next floor to her apartment.

When she walked in, Zep met her at the door. She bent down and picked him up and he licked her face. They played together for a little while and then Landry turned on some music and cleaned up the kitchen. She washed the coffeepot and set it to turn on in the morning. She went into her small office and checked all of her emails. She had a lot of them. Some were from business contacts and some were personal ones. She responded to all that needed attention and deleted the rest of them. Zep had jumped up into her lap and was snoring. She smiled and got her tiny recorder from her purse. She rewound it and played back everything she had recorded that day so she wouldn't forget anything. When she was done, she put the recorder on the desk and sat there for a minute before she had to wake Zep up. She remembered that Ms. Millie was coming back to the bookstore tomorrow and Landry wanted to go over there and check on her. She had a feeling that it was not going to go well.

Instead of sitting on the balcony, which was her usual ritual at night before bed, she decided to call Annie. She and Zep went into the den and she turned the tv on low. She dialed and Annie picked up right away. "Hello, my best friend. How's it going" Annie said.

Landry smiled into the phone. "Not dancing as much as usual. It's not as much fun without you here laughing at me." she replied to Annie.

She heard a sigh and Annie said, "I know. I miss you so much, too. Especially since Blaine is out of the picture now. He at least kept me occupied so that I didn't pout about you moving away. Why did you have to go and do that, Lan?"

"You know why, Annie. I will never in my lifetime have the chance to own my own business...much less, two of them. Boy, was I shocked about inheriting this apartment building." she laughed, "But, you know what? I am enjoying all of it. I worked Ms. Millie shifts at the bookstore this week and I really enjoyed it. I was actually missing my time at the library but helping customers find books that interest them and shelving some new books we were delivered made me happy. I think I am going to make this gig work pretty well." She chuckled.

"I am happy for you. I really am. But, I am sad for me. I feel like a lost puppy whose owner abandoned her. I don't know what to do with myself unless I am at work. There, I just run on automatic and put out fires all day. After work, I pick up the phone to call you and see what we are going to get into. Then I remember that you don't live here anymore. I think this is what it is like to be miserable."

Landry frowned. "Oh, Annie. I am so sorry you feel that bad. Surely, there is someone you can hang out with and have some fun with. I mean, I know I am special and all, but somebody should be able to replace me."

Annie said, "Nope. Nobody. They just don't get me and all the inside jokes you and I had for so many years.

Anyway, don't worry about me. I will get myself adjusted one of these days soon. I think it is mostly because you and Blaine left me close to the same time." She laughed and told Landry that she had to get going because she had beans boiling and the water had evaporated out of them and they were burning. Just then, Landry heard the smoke alarm in the background, laughed and told her goodbye.

She looked at Zep. "She's right, ya know. She and I are both klutzes. That's why we clicked in the first place." She picked up Zep, turned the tv off and they headed to bed. As Landry lay there after she said her prayers, she still thought there was something important that she was not remembering. She couldn't for the life of her remember the conversation or who she had it with. She drifted off to sleep still thinking about it.

Chapter 21

The next morning, Landry got her a cup of coffee and looked outside on the balcony. It was already raining and it was supposed to rain even harder as the day and night wore on. She looked down at Zep who, naturally, was watching her every move. "Sorry, bud. You will have to use your pads today. Not a good day for you to go walking, especially with you being so low to the ground and all." She laughed. Zep did not.

She gave him some fresh food and water and then grabbed her a bowl of cereal before going into the den. She turned on the weather and they were still saying heavy rains throughout the day and night. She watched the local news and turned the tv off just as her phone was ringing. It was Lisa telling her that the security company was there and was beginning to install the cameras. The process would take all day but they were confident they would get them all installed.

Landry thanked her for the update and decided to get dressed for the day. She had ordered something for Ms. Millie at the jewelry store and wanted to pick it up before she went to see her at the bookstore. She was actually longing to see Ms. Millie but, at the same time, she was dreading her reaction. She hoped that Ms. Millie wasn't still mad at her about the mushroom incident.

Her phone rang as she was just about ready to leave. It was Adam. He asked if she had anything planned for lunch.

He told her that he was craving a burger and shake from Takeout King and thought they might meet there. She told him that she had a few things to do today but that she should be free around lunchtime. They agreed on the time and hung up. She told Zep goodbye and made sure to get her umbrella.

When she went through the lobby, the installers were busy putting up the security cameras. She spoke to them in passing and then stopped at Lisa's desk. "I feel better already getting those put in." Lisa nodded and said that she agreed.

They both turned when they heard Garrett grumble. "What is it, Garrett? Is something wrong?" Landry asked him.

"No Miss Burke. Well, it's just that I hope all of this new technology won't be the end of my job. I believe that a human and personal touch is necessary to make people feel at ease."

"Garrett. First of all, security cameras are hardly new technology. I was very surprised that Aunt Tildie didn't have them installed here already. Secondly, I think I have made it clear that I am more comfortable with 24/7 coverage by our lobby assistants than anyone else. Your job is not in danger; anyone who works here has job security. I hope you understand that." Landry told him.

"Very well, Miss Burke. Ah…thank you for that reassurance." He walked away.

Landry turned to Lisa. "I have an errand to run and then I am going to attempt to make peace with Ms. Millie.

Wish me luck."

She walked down the street to the jewelry store. When she walked in, Mr. Griffith, the manager, greeted her. "Hello, Miss Burke. We have your package all ready for you." He went to the back and brought it out.

"This is lovely, Mr. Griffith. Just perfect." she told him.

"Please call me Harrison, Miss Burke. I hope we can do business again soon. I put this on your account and will send the invoice at the end of the month. Thank you for purchasing from us."

"You are very welcome, Harrison. I love the customer service you provide here." She turned and left, picking up her wet umbrella from outside the front door.

When she walked into the bookstore, she heard Ms. Millie yell from the back office. "Come on in and out of that rain. I will be right with you." She knew then that Ms. Millie had not seen who had entered. Not with that cheery and kind greeting. She was right because when Ms. Millie walked up front and saw her, she threw both of her hands in front of her and made the sign of the cross with her fingers.

"Don't come near me, Landry. I am feeling better but I am not up to any of your foolishness. I can't go through another trauma right now. Go pick on somebody else."

Landry's shoulders sank and she got tears in her eyes. "Ms. Millie, you have to know that I had no idea you were allergic to mushrooms. If I did, I wouldn't have put them in that quiche. It was supposed to be a peace offering as it was. I am so very sorry but, please don't push me out of your life. I don't think I could bear that."

"Stop. You are just trying to get my guard down again. I have learned that I have to be prepared when you are around. Why didn't Tildie tell me you were dangerous? She always talked about how sweet and kind you were. You are those things but, I declare Landry, every time I am around you something bad seems to happen to me." Ms. Millie was shaking her head like she was confused or something.

Landry had gotten angry now. "I know, Ms. Millie, but I don't do anything to make that happen. It just does. I am sweet and kind. I am also respectful, intelligent and caring. Do you actually think that I came over here with that quiche thinking, 'Oh, I bet Ms. Millie is allergic to mushrooms. Let me see if I can send her into anaphylactic shock?' Or, when we went to the yard sale, I said to myself, 'I bet this empty lounge chair with nobody anywhere near it is for people to get their faces painted. Let me put Ms. Millie there and tell her to rest so that some person can catch her sleeping and paint her face.' No, Ms. Millie, I did not." Landry looked her right in the eyes. "I treasure our friendship and I never want it to end but, if you feel like I am targeting you for some reason, I guess I can get Lisa to run interference as far as business goes. We won't have to interact with each other anymore."

Ms. Millie stood there like a stone. When she finally blinked her eyes, it was to push the tears out that came streaming down her face. "You are a crazy child. I have loved you since you were just a little girl. All in the world I want is to take care of you for Tildie and keep you safe. I am scared to death that one of these days you are going to do something to get yourself hurt and that would kill me. Now, get over here and hug me and try not to push me down in the process." She smiled.

They hugged it out and Landry remembered her gift. She gave it to Ms. Millie and told her to open it. Ms. Millie looked at the box for a second and said, "Well, it looks too small to hold a piece of dynamite that will blow me up, so I guess I will take a chance and open it"

Landry made a face at her and stuck out her tongue. Ms. Millie laughed and opened the box. It was a medical bracelet. It had a place to list things you are allergic to in case you have a reaction. The medical professionals could see it and treat you accordingly. Landry had them engrave "mushrooms" on it. Ms. Millie smiled and said it was the kindest gift she had ever received.

"Is there anything else you are allergic to?" Landry asked her. "If so, just run by the jewelry store and ask Mr. Griffith to engrave it on there and charge it to me. He has my billing info already."

Ms. Millie looked her dead in the eye and said, "There is one more thing…I am allergic to people trying to kill me."

Landry gathered up her purse and umbrella and walked out. She turned around when she got outside and saw Ms. Millie laughing and slapping her thigh with her hand. Landry knew everything was alright between them again.

When she got back to Magnolia Place, she noticed the town newspaper in the rack in front of the building. They had published some pictures from the high school prom. There on the cover, in living color, was Jenna and her date. Jenna glowed in her gorgeous blue prom dress with shoes to match. She also had a corsage on her shoulder and her date's tie and boutonniere matched Jenna's dress. That made Landry's heart sing and she was so pleased with the smile on Jenna's face.

Landry ducked under the security guys and went up to her apartment. She still had some time before she was to meet Adam for lunch. She spoke to Zep as she walked in and decided to put some laundry in to wash. That done, she put on some music and danced around as she swept the kitchen and unloaded the dishwasher. Since it was going to be raining all night, she wanted to get her chores done so that she and Zep could get comfortable and lay down early. She had a brand new book she wanted to start and tonight would be the perfect night for it.

Just as she sat down to rest, Judith called her from the B&B. She told Landry that she had made and served the Possum Pie last night for her guests and it was a huge hit. She said it was a wonderful conversation starter and that some of the men got into long conversations about hunting and fishing before the meal was over. She said their wives shook their heads and asked for the recipe. Judith wanted to know if it would be alright for her to give it to them.

"Of course it would." Landry replied. "I am so glad that it was a hit. You know, I have another pie recipe with an unusual name. I will have to get that one to you, too."

"I would love that. Thank you so much. I have to run

to make lunch now but I just wanted you to know how much they loved it." Judith hung up.

The intercom buzzed just then. Landry walked over and answered it. Lisa said, "Landry, I hate to ask but are you going back out today?" Landry said that she was going out for lunch. Lisa asked her if she could please take the deposits from Magnolia Place and Jasmine Bloom to the bank. She said she always took Ms. Millie's deposit when she took the checks from the residents for the rent but that she didn't want to leave today since the security people were there.

"Sure. I will leave a few minutes early and take them. No problem."

Lisa thanked her and said that Garrett was running over to the bookstore to pick up Ms. Milie's deposit so they would both be with Lisa when Landry was ready to go.

Landry finished up her chores and got dressed. Since it was such a yucky day, she wore jeans and a thin sweatshirt and her boots. She braided her hair down her back since she knew the wet weather would wreak havoc on it. She made sure that Zep had food and water and put him in the den with the tv on low. She grabbed her purse and umbrella and left. She picked up the deposits from Lisa and was turning to go to the garage when she saw Penney Goode get out of the elevator. Landry asked her how prom had gone.

"It was great,' Penney said. "We had a wonderful time and lots of kids attended."

"Do you by any chance know Jenna Shipman?" Landry asked.

"Um, yeah. I know Jenna. She works over at Jasmine Bloom, right?" Penney looked a little unsure.

"She does." Replied Landry. "I know that she attended prom, too. I saw her picture on the front of the newspaper. Her dress was lovely, don't you think, Penney?"

"Yes, I thought it was gorgeous. I was happy to see her at Prom. She doesn't attend many events that we have at school. I have to hurry. I have classes this afternoon and with the rain and all, I will have to drive slowly. Nice to see you, Miss Burke." Landry told her goodbye and to be careful on the wet roads. Then, she headed to the bank.

She parked her car and went inside since the drive-thru was closed for repairs. She waited her turn and when she was called, it was by Hannah Torres. She stepped up to the counter and said, "Hannah, right? I have seen you before here but I didn't know then that you are Lisa's roommate. It is so nice to see you again."

Hannah smiled and said, "Hi, Miss Burke. Lisa has said so many nice things about you. She loves working for you so much." Landry told Hannah to call her by her first name and that she hoped they could all get together one night for dinner soon. They completed the deposit transactions and Landry left to go back out into the rain to go to her car. That is when she bumped right into a woman who was running into the bank with her head down since he didn't have an umbrella to keep the rain off of her. Landry looked up to apologize for bumping into her and saw that the woman was Portia Roy. Landry opened the door for her and followed her back into the bank.

"Portia, right?" she asked. Portia whipped her head around so fast at the mention of her name that rain water sprayed off of her hair into the air. "Yes. Can I help you?" Landry heard Wyatt's words in her head telling her to not get involved with the investigation but, at the same time, she felt that this was personal and she just had to question Portia if she could.

"I heard you singing at the Sky High one night and I loved your voice. You are very good." Portia blushed and thanked her for the compliment. Landry continued, "I was wondering if we could talk for just a minute. My name is Landry Burke."

She saw the reaction in Portia's eyes. It was like a deer caught in the headlights. Portia responded, "I am in a hurry right now. My waitressing shift starts at the Purple Cactus in half an hour. I really can't be late."

Landry thought fast and said, "I completely understand. I have a lunch appointment that I need to get to also. It won't take long at all if you could just give me a couple of minutes." She led Portia over to two chairs with a small table between them that sat out of the main flow of the bank. Portia reluctantly sat down and asked what Landry needed from her.

"That night that I saw you sing was the night that Melodie Leiton burst in and accused you of killing her brother or knowing who did. Why would she say something like that?" Landry looked intently at Portia to gauge her reaction to the question. She hoped that she could find out something that would help find Fred's killer.

Portia responded, "I have no idea. I mean, Fred and I dated for a very short time but that was over ages ago. We just weren't good together. I have a new boyfriend now and before you ask, I had absolutely nothing to do with Melodie's murder. I was shocked about it. She and I never got along but I would never kill anybody. Melodie was involved in lots of things over the years. I guess some of it finally caught up with her."

"Why would she think you would know who killed Fred? He was killed in my building and was one of my employees. He seemed like a quiet loner to those who worked with him and even the people he went to school with years ago. They all said that he kept to himself and didn't socialize much at all. Does that sound like the Fred you dated?"

"Pretty much." Portia admitted. "He and Melodie were complete opposites. In fact, one of the reasons Fred and I didn't work out was that he didn't like going out and wanted to stay home all the time. With me being an entertainer, I have to go out all the time. We just didn't click." She stood up, "Sorry, Miss Burke. I have to go now or I will be late for my shift. I really don't know anything else. Goodbye."

As Portia walked up to the counter to conduct her business, Landry went out to her car. She hadn't gotten any information out of Portia that was very helpful.

When she got to the Takeout King, Adam was sitting in his car waiting for her. He ran over and opened her door as she put her umbrella up. As they walked in the door, she said, "I had no idea they had a dining room here. With the name being 'Takeout King', I thought they only had a drive thru and maybe a counter inside to order. I thought we were going to eat it in the car." Adam laughed and said, "Well, this place has been here almost since the town was founded, I think. For years and years it was just takeout as the name implies. Then, when Mr. Tillson bought it, he expanded it to include an area to dine in."

They took their seats at a table and looked at the menus. Adam ordered a cheeseburger all the way and homemade fries. He got a rootbeer float to drink. Landry ordered a foot long chili cheese dog with tater tots and a diet soda. "This place is amazing." She said, "There is a drive in diner in Bent Branch that serves almost the same things as here. It has been there for over 60 years. Annie and I went there alot and ate in our car and talked. They have the most delicious hot fudge cakes you have ever tasted and still have waiters and waitresses that skate to your car with your order. I miss those times with Annie. She is the best friend I have ever had and it was so hard leaving her. We saw each other every single day and talked on the phone several times a day."

"It must be hard for you. Maybe she can come for a visit or you can visit her soon. I am lucky since Wyatt is my best friend and neither one of us has any desire to leave here. Of course, I'm sure you didn't want to leave Bent Branch, either, until this opportunity fell in your lap." Adam turned at the sound of his name. "Well, Mr. Wilcox. Good to see you. Uh…and you, too, Miss Burke." the booming voice said.

"Hello Mr. Mayor." Adam answered.

Landry just smiled and nodded towards Mayor Cartwright. He sat down at their table without asking. "Miss Burke, I think I owe you an apology. My wife and The Pink Hat Ladies Group informed me that they had a wonderful event at Magnolia Place. Barb said that everything was perfect and that it was the best event they have ever had. Miss Burke, I think you may have misunderstood me when we had our last conversation. I in no way intended to suggest that you were personally responsible for the death in your building. I was just overcome with shock that we had a murder in our fine town. Of course, we later had another one and I understand that you also found the body in that one, too."

Landry looked at Mayor Cartwright. "Yes, Mayor, I unfortunately did. I guess your 'fine town' as you call it didn't send out a very nice welcome wagon to introduce me to my new town. You will have to do better with that." Adam's eyes got big and Mayor Cartwright's face got red.

"Yes, well, I have to go now. I see a constituent that is motioning me to come over. Good day to you both." He got up and walked away very fast.

"Probably saw someone who would buy his lunch. You ever heard the expression 'deep pockets, short arms'? That's our Mayor. I think he is in shock. Most people don't stand up to him like you did. They try to make nice with the Mayor of the town in case they ever need a favor." Adam told her.

Landry shrugged and said, "That's just not me. I am who I am, like it or not. Remember, I was a librarian for years before I left that job. I don't believe in censorship…not even from me."

Their food was delivered then and they both dug into the wonderful meal. They were about halfway done when Wyatt walked in the door. "Well, well. Imagine seeing you two here. What's good today? Mind if I sit down?" He took off his Sheriff's hat and hung it on the empty chair.

"Of course not. How has it been going, Wyatt?" Landry asked. Wyatt let out a loud breath, lowered his voice and said, "Lee and Scat are not talking. Zilch. Both have lawyered up and, even though we have Lee dead to right for Melodie's murder, he won't say who else is involved. We are still looking for Fred's murderer. I interviewed Portia Roy again, hoping she would break. She is Scat's girlfriend and she has to know something but wouldn't cough anything up. She denied knowing anything about any of it. I'll be honest, that girl seems like a nice person. I have no idea why she would be involved with the Garrison brothers. They have been bad news their whole life." He ordered a cheeseburger and a lemonade from their waiter.

"I have to say I agree. I spoke to her at the bank today and got the same impression of her. Did you two know that she and Fred dated for awhile?" Landry asked Wyatt and Adam.

"Yeah. That didn't last long." Adam said. "I think she and Fred were more suited than her and Carl Garrison. I mean, his nickname is Scat. That says something right there." They all laughed and then Wyatt looked at Landry. "I thought I asked you politely to stay out of this investigation. What were you doing talking to Portia Roy about it? You know that she is dating the brother of one of our murderers. Landry, this is dangerous stuff. You have to be very careful what you say to suspects. Something wrong and it could get you killed." He shook his head as his food was set in front of him.

"I understand that, Wyatt. I just asked her why Melodie accused her of knowing who killed Fred. That's all. She said she had no idea and that was that. I was really just making conversation." she said sweetly.

"Uh-huh. And, I am Captain Kangaroo. I mean it, Landry. Stop interfering in this. We have leads that you don't even know about because I can't tell you or anyone else about them. Just trust me to do my job." Wyatt wolfed down his food and said he had to go. He grabbed his hat off of the back of the chair and said, "Things to do and places to be. Look, Landry, you are my friend and I don't want to ruin that by saying something rude. Just please stay out of it, ok?"

"I will. I promise. In fact after I leave there, I am heading home for the day. It is supposed to rain even harder tonight and I have a brand new book to read. Zep and I have a date tonight with popcorn, doggie treats and my book." She told him.

Wyatt smiled as he walked out shaking his head. He put that big hat back on and ran out into the rain.

As Adam and Landry were leaving, the rain picked up. There was thunder and lightning now, too. Adam walked Landry to her car and they spoke under the umbrellas they were carrying.

"Are you really going home for the day?" Adam asked.

Landry laughed and said, "Yep. That's the plan. I just feel the need to rest a little and this is the perfect day for it. I don't want to be sloshing around in this mess, anyway. How about you? Do you have plans for the rest of the day?"

"Nope. I am going over to Mom's and spend a little time with her then I am going to head home myself. This kind of weather makes me lazy." He chuckled. "See ya later, Landry. Make sure to lock your doors when you get home. Can't be too careful."

She promised that she would and got in her Bug to head home. As she walked out of the garage at Magnolia Place and went into the lobby, she saw that the security camera crew was still working. She walked up to Lisa's desk and asked her, "Are they still working here in the lobby? I thought they would have been done down here by now and would be up on the floors or over at Jasmine Bloom."

"Oh, they put the two cameras down here and then went upstairs and completed all of the work up there. They just got back from the bookstore and those are already done. They said they are adjusting the ones in the lobby and will then work on the ones in the grill area and garage." Lisa told her.

"I guess I didn't realize how much work is involved in doing this. Sounds like they have it under control. I am in for the day, Lisa. I'm going to make it an early night tonight."

"Gotcha." Lisa snapped her fingers and said, "Oh, I meant to tell you that Zack called and he won't be in for his shift tonight. His wife was hurting really bad on the right side of her abdomen earlier today. He took her to the hospital and found out it was her appendix. He is there now waiting for her to get out of surgery. He said he will see us Monday if that is alright."

"Of course. I will be praying for everything to go well with the surgery and recovery. That's scary and I am sure glad he was there when it happened." Landry said.

She thought for a second and said, "Have you asked Orvis if he would like to cover Zack's shift tonight? I know he only works on weekends, but he might like to get the extra hours."

"I thought of that and called Orvis at the dealership in Wrigley Springs. He said he would love to but he can't. He promised his friend that he would help him load up things from his house since he and his wife are moving tomorrow. Orvis said his friend had a covered patio, so they are going to park the moving truck there and put the things from the house in it. Orvis is staying the night with them but he said to tell you that he will be here in the morning at 9am for his regular shift."

Landry pointed out the window and said, "With how hard they say it is going to rain tonight, I don't think we will have many people out and about tonight anyway. Don't worry about it, Lisa. It will be fine with Zack not here. As a matter of fact, when you are caught up, go ahead and leave for home before it gets any worse out there. I told Ms. Millie to go home when the cameras were installed and I see that she has already left. I sent a text to both Jenna and Maisy to take the afternoon off. They say the thunderstorms that are coming in tonight are going to be very strong." She turned, spoke to the installers and went upstairs.

Chapter 22

Zep was in the den on the couch sleeping when she got to the apartment. She looked at his bowl and he had eaten all of his food, as well as the two treats she had left there. She sat on the couch and picked him up. He licked her face and whined like she had been gone for weeks instead of hours. She cuddled and played with him for awhile and then got up and changed his puppy pads. She also put down clean water and food for him and then decided to get into her pj's for the night. She put on a pair of thin, comfy pants and added a thicker long sleeved shirt and some socks. She left her hair braided for the night and found her new book in the living room. She and Zep went into the bedroom and snuggled in under the comforter. She was still full from lunch, so she bypassed the planned popcorn for now.

The thunder was so loud that both she and Zep jumped when it clapped. She got up and walked to the living room and looked out of the balcony window. The rain was getting heavier and the lightning was very sharp. Landry was very glad that she didn't have to be out there in this and hoped everyone else in the building would be safe. She was the only one at home on her floor since Karen Scott was still away and Glenn Mayhew wasn't in either. She assumed that he was busy in another part of his district. The company he worked for sure seemed dependable and it was obvious that they were very hard workers. She hated the thought of them having to get on the roads later tonight when they were done with the installing of the cameras. Right then, her phone rang and it was Adam.

"Just wanted to be sure you stuck to your decision to stay home tonight. I didn't stay long at Mom's. The weather got so much worse after I got there, that she ran me off." He laughed. "She told me to get home and off of the roads. You know, we don't have that many hurricanes in this part of Tennessee but they say that this weather is coming from the hurricane that hit the outer banks of North Carolina and moved inland. These rains are coming from the outer bands of that storm. Pretty wicked weather. I sure don't want to be out in it."

"Me, either. I hope Wyatt and his deputies stay safe. You know there will probably be road accidents with this kind of weather. I heard sirens a few minutes ago passing by this building." Landry said.

Adam assured her that it would be alright. He said he hated it for all of the emergency personnel that had to go out on calls in weather like this, but that they are experienced at what they do and would be fine. He told Landry that he was going to heat up some chili that Judith had sent home with him and, if the signal held out, he was going to watch some baseball on tv. After that, he would probably be going to bed early. They said goodnight and Landry went back to the bedroom.

Zep was snoring and Landry opened her book and started reading. It was a very good book and she didn't want to put it down. When she woke up to the ringing of her phone, the book was laying open on her chest. She looked at the number on her phone and didn't recognize it but, since she hadn't programmed all of the residents phone numbers in yet, she answered it anyway. A woman's voice said, "Is this Landry?"

"Yes it is. How may I help you?"

"Landry, this is Sylvia Weathers from the Art Gallery. I am so sorry to disturb you but, I had a conversation with someone today at the Gallery and it has bothered me ever since. I think I may have some information that can help solve Fred's murder." Sylvia sounded breathless. "I have been riding around in this horrible weather mulling the conversation over in my mind. I can't even sleep because I am so worried about it. I don't want to go to the Sheriff with what I think I know until I am sure that I am right. It would be horrible to accuse someone without knowing if I misunderstood what they said to me. I also know that the Sheriff and all of his deputies are probably running ragged with this terrible weather. Surely, they will have extra work tonight. I know I sound like a crazy person but you are the only one I can think of to talk to about this. I mean, Fred was killed in your building and you also had a painting stolen from that same building. I know you must want this solved soon. Do you think I could come over and tell you what I heard and then we can decide if this is as important as I think it is?"

"Of course you can discuss this with me, Sylvia, but the weather is awful right now and truthfully, I was asleep when you called. Surely this can wait until tomorrow. I will make us something to eat and you can come over then and we will figure it out." Landry said.

"Oh, Landry. I won't sleep a wink until I tell someone about this. I hate to think that a killer is on the loose and I might have information that will reveal who it is. I guess I could go ahead and call Sheriff Collins. I just hate to bother him if I am not sure this information is relevant. I heard today that he is following up on every single lead himself. I know how bad he wants to get this case solved."

Landry thought she heard the elevator door open on her floor but she knew that the other two residents were not in town. It made her a little uneasy and she thought to herself that maybe she would like some company after all.

"You know what, Sylvia? Come on over. I will put some coffee on and once you tell me what you heard and we decide that Wyatt needs to know, we can call and ask him to drop by. Does that sound alright?" Landry asked her.

Sylvia said it sounded perfect and Landry said, "Oh, and Sylvia? If the lobby doors are locked like they should be, call me back when you are in front of the doors and I will buzz you in. They will automatically lock when you close them back." Sylvia agreed and hung up.

Landry went into the kitchen and turned on the coffee pot. She walked back to her bedroom and since Zep was still sleeping, she decided to close the door and leave him in there. She didn't want him whining and jumping on Sylvia since she didn't know how she felt about dogs. She went into the bathroom and looked in the mirror. She decided to leave her hair braided and also to keep her pj's on. They were really just a pair of thin sweats and a shirt, anyway, and she planned to go right back to sleep when Sylvia left. As she left the bathroom to go back to the living room, she glanced down the hallway and saw that she had left the little lamp on in her office. She went in to turn it off and there lay her tiny recorder where she had left it the night before. Good thing she didn't need it while she was out today, she thought, and picked it up and put it in the front pocket of her sweats. She would put it back in her purse when she went back to the bedroom to go to sleep later.

Her phone rang and it was Sylvia telling her she was at the front door of the lobby. Landry could hear the rain pouring and the thunder raging over the phone. She pushed the little button by the intercom and buzzed Sylvia in. Landry heard the doors close behind Sylvia before she hung up the phone. "Do you know where my apartment is?"

Sylvia asked if Landry was in Miss Tildie's old apartment and Landry when said yes, Sylvia said she knew which one it was. A few minutes later, there was a knock on her door and she let Sylvia, who was soaking wet, in the apartment. Landry went into the bathroom and got a towel and brought it out for Sylvia to dry off. "Thank you so much." Sylvia said. "It started raining even harder while I was standing out front and the wind got up so much it blew it all over me." Landry noticed that Sylvia was shaking and her teeth were chattering.

"Would you like some coffee to warm you up a little?"

she asked. Sylvia said that would be wonderful and Landry went into the kitchen to get them both a cup. While she was doing that, Sylvia yelled to her, "I will be so glad when this case is solved. I have been worried to death that someone will evade my security at the Art Gallery and steal some of my expensive paintings. It is just dreadful to think about."

At that moment, Landry stopped pouring the coffee and stood staring at the wall. She finally remembered the conversation that she had been trying to think of for weeks. Where was her cell phone? She remembered she had left it on the table in the living room by the door. Now what? "Think, Landry, think." she thought to herself. She decided that she would pick the phone up and tell Sylvia that she had to take it to the office to charge it. Then, she would call Wyatt.

She picked up the coffee mugs to take to the living room and tried to stop her shaking and heavy breathing. When she felt like she was calm enough, she turned around and there stood Sylvia in the doorway of the kitchen with a gun pointed right at her. "Put the mugs down, Landry, and walk slowly to the living room."

Landry put the mugs on the kitchen table and as she walked past Sylvia, she reached in her pocket and turned on the tiny recorder there. She could only hope that it would record what was being said clear enough through her thin sweatpants. She sat down and spoke way more calmly than she felt, "Why did you do it, Sylvia?"

"I realized I had made a mistake during our conversation at the Gallery. I knew it was only a matter of time before you remembered what we said and would pick up on my faux pas. I can't let you go to the Sheriff with what you know. You will ruin my entire operation and I have worked too hard to see it crumble. Besides, I have no intention of spending even a day in a grimy, dirty jail cell."

"I actually didn't remember our conversation until just now when I was in the kitchen and you were speaking to me. Something you said reminded me of it. At the Gallery, you told me that the painting of Aunt Tildie's that had been stolen was the most expensive one you had curated for any of your clients. But, the Sheriff's Department or anyone else never said which painting was stolen. They purposely didn't say which one because of the ongoing investigation. So, the only way you could have known that it was the most expensive painting is if you stole it yourself or told someone else which one to take." Landry started breathing heavily and was twisting her ring very fast. She told herself that she could not afford to have a panic attack right now. She had to keep calm. She took some deep breaths and said, "Sylvia, why did you kill Fred?"

Sylvia sat on the sofa and kept the gun pointing right at Landry as she said, "I guess there's no reason not to tell you the entire story since you will be dead soon." Landry started shaking all over and Sylvia got an evil smile on her face like she was glad that Landry was scared out of her wits.

"You see, my brother, Victor, and I run this operation. He lives in Europe and finds buyers for the paintings our employees steal. We steal paintings that I or one of our cohorts sold. See, we get paid when we sell it the first time and then we steal it back and get paid all over again when we sell it on the black market. It was going wonderfully until I was foolish enough to hire these local idiots to help me. I have contacts and employees all over the country but I needed someone locally when we needed to get to some paintings that were worth high dollar on the black market. Fred, Lee, Melodie and Scat were all part of my business." she laughed.

"After Miss Tildie passed away, I had to get my hands on that painting of hers. I called Fred one day and told him that I needed him to get me in the event room that evening. I knew he might balk at helping me to steal Miss Tildie's painting since he was so fond of her, so I told him I needed to just go in and take a picture of the painting for insurance purposes since I forgot to do that before she died. He told me to ask Lisa since she was the manager of the building. Of course, I knew I couldn't do that so I gave him a song and dance about not wanting to get in trouble for not documenting things as I should have when I sold the painting. I offered him a huge bonus to get me in that room. He finally agreed and said for me to meet him here after his shift ended at 8pm. There was no other person coming in to relieve him since the building didn't have 24/7 coverage then." She looked very proud of herself at that moment.

Sylvia put the gun in her other hand and aimed it back at Landry. She sighed like she was bored of telling this story, but continued. "I arrived at 9pm. He and I went up the stairs. I didn't want to run into any of the other residents that may be using the elevators and Fred was used to taking the stairs anyway. We got to the Event Room and I put on my gloves that I used when I handled any painting so as not to get oil from my hands on them. I took out my camera, then I faked becoming dizzy. I sat down and told Fred that I thought my sugar was too low and asked if he would check the fridge in the kitchen to see if there was any orange juice or soda left in there. He went into the kitchen and I got the painting off of the wall and put it beside the door. He came back in and saw what I was doing and started chasing me screaming that I could not steal Miss Tildie's painting. I ran into the kitchen and grabbed a knife from a drawer. He charged me and I stabbed him in the chest. He fell immediately to the floor. I waited until I knew he was dead before I left. I was going back into the Event Room when I looked down and noticed that I had Fred's blood on one of the gloves. I ran to the bathroom and put the gloves in my purse and washed up."

"So Fred died protecting my aunt's prized possession. How could you be so cold hearted, Sylvia? He was a good man." Landry felt so sorry for Fred. He was loyal to Aunt Tildie even after her death.

Sylvia laughed. "He may have been but remember, he also worked for me. He helped to transport paintings that were stolen. He would hide close by when Scat or Lee was stealing a painting and have that beat up old truck running so that they could make a fast getaway."

The thunder clapped hard outside and the lightning lit up the room. They both screamed at the same time from the booming of the thunder. Landry adjusted her body a little hoping that would help the recorder work better. At least, if she died, Wyatt and Adam would know what happened and could tell her Mom and Annie.

"What about Melodie? What part did she play?" Landry asked as she twisted her ring and prayed that someone would come by before Sylvia killed her.

"Landry, I know you are just trying to extend your life by asking all these questions but I will play your little game a while longer. Melodie was the biggest player of them all. When she couldn't be a 'groupie' as she called it anymore, she happened to bump into me at the grocery store one day. She walked out with me and casually asked if I needed any help at the gallery. I laughed, of course. Can you even imagine her type working around my clientele? I told her as much and then said that I had a side business that she would fit into better. I explained what was needed and she jumped at the chance. I pay very well, by the way." She actually looked proud.

Landry could hear what sounded like sirens on the street below and prayed that it was someone coming to rescue her, although she feared it was a car wreck that brought them out in this weather. Sylvia sneezed about that time but never lost a grip on the gun. She didn't seem to notice the sirens.

"Anyway," Sylvia continued, "I purchased an RV and we stored it at a storage facility outside of Nashville where many singers and bands store their buses when they aren't on the road. When we got a fix on a painting that we could steal, Lee and Scat took instructions from me and stole it. Fred would be waiting in the truck and they would take the painting to the storage facility in Nashville and place it in the RV. When I had worked with Victor to establish who wanted to purchase it, Melodie would drive to the storage facility and wrap the painting with the materials that I had in the RV for her. She would then leave her car there and drive the RV to a middleman that my brother had arranged. Sometimes, we had several paintings at a time. She drove all over the country. We make millions of dollars a year." she bragged.

"Why was Melodie killed?" Landry decided that, even if Sylvia was going to kill her, she wanted to get what she could on tape so that Sylvia would be arrested.

Sylvia laughed and her voice got even more evil. "That little tramp got greedy. She had three paintings to deliver the week before she came back to Bobwhite Mountain. She delivered two of them and then called me on her way back to Nashville to tell me that she had stopped to get something to eat at a truckstop on her way to deliver the third one. She claimed that while she was inside, someone broke into the RV and stole it. Of course, I knew she was lying and that she had sold it at a pawn shop or somewhere else to make a little extra money for herself. I told Lee about it and told him that the painting she had 'lost' was his and Scat's pay for the month. He is a hothead and went to confront her and he killed her."

"One more question, Sylvia. What about Portia? Melodie seemed to think that she knew who had killed

Fred. How was she involved with your scheme?"

"That one is not the brightest bulb in the box. She didn't even know she was involved. You see, she was at the Sky High one night after her set and overheard the Pugh's talking about their butler being out of town. Lucy told Brad that she had told their housemaids that they were welcome to go to the top floor of the home to watch movies since they were there alone that night. Brad said something like, "Good. They will enjoy themselves." Portia left for a date with Scat. She was making conversation and trying to think of something to say when she told him about what she had overheard. She was basically saying that it must be nice to have a movie theater in your home. Scat told her he was tired and needed to go home and get some rest. Of course, he called me since he knew there was a painting in the Pugh's home that I had been eyeing to steal. He and Lee broke in and got the painting with no problem."

Landry heard Zep whining in the bedroom. She hoped that he would settle back down because she didn't want Sylvia to hurt him. Sylvia jumped up and pointed the gun at Landry's head and said, "Ok. Enough stalling. Out on the balcony. Now."

Landry was surprised that Sylvia wanted to go on the balcony. It was pouring rain and the wind was blowing the water onto the balcony. The storm was just getting worse. She did what she was told to do, though, and with every step she felt like she was walking to her death. She was breathing heavily and was saying the Lord's Prayer in her mind. She was ready if He was ready for her but if He wasn't, she was going to fight with everything she had.

They got on the balcony and Sylvia told her to back up against the railing. "What are you going to do, Syliva? Please don't kill me. I don't care about what you are doing with these paintings. I just want to live. I won't say a word of what you told me."

Sylvia laughed out loud. "You certainly won't. You see, you are going to jump to your death. All the pressure of a new town and new responsibilities was just too much for you. Your stress and anxiety was overwhelming and you couldn't take it anymore, so you jumped."

That got Landry's attention. She jerked her knee up and into Sylvia's hand. The gun flew out of her hand and over the railing. Landry saw an evil look in Sylvia's eyes at that moment and then felt her head being pushed backwards over the railing by Sylvia, who had her palm squarely on Landry's chin and was pushing with all of her might. Then she put both of her hands on Landry's neck and started squeezing. Landry turned and twisted until she got out of that predicament but Sylvia was determined. She grabbed Landry's one of Landry's legs over pushed it over the rail. Landry was fighting with all of her might to not go over the rail when all of a sudden she heard, "Stop, Sylvia. Get away from her."

Sylvia was stunned and loosened her grip on Landry. When she looked up and could focus, Landry saw Wyatt and every deputy on the force pointing their weapons at Sylvia. Knowing she was defeated, Sylvia started to climb the railing to jump. Wyatt reached his big arm around her and wrestled her down. "Oh, no, Syliva. You are not going to take the easy way out." The next thing Landry knew, Sylvia was in handcuffs on the floor of her living room and being read her rights.

Someone had Landry in their arms and carried her to the sofa in the living room and wrapped a blanket around her. She looked up and looked into the clearest, bluest eyes she had ever seen. Adam was there. She promptly passed out.

Chapter 23

When she came to, Adam was still staring at her but there was another man checking her injuries. It was Logan Watson from the 3rd floor of the building. Adam had remembered that Landry had told him about Logan doing his Residency at the hospital. He looked up and told her that she seemed to be fine. Nothing was broken, but she would have some pretty bruises on her tomorrow.

"Thank you so much, Logan. I am sorry we disturbed you so late. I hope it didn't wake the twins up." Landry pushed herself up on the pillow that was under her head.

"Oh, no. They sleep through most anything now. I was actually up when Adam knocked on our door. I have several patients assigned to me at the hospital and I was doing some updates on my notes." Logan said goodbye and got up to leave.

Landry sat up and saw so many people in her apartment that she didn't know where to look first. Someone sat a hot cup of coffee on the table beside the sofa and she grabbed it and guzzled it down so fast that she started to choke. She had never been so happy to be surrounded by people. Sylvia had been taken away by deputies.

Wyatt came over and sat down beside her. "We are locking her up for attempted murder right now. I hope you can remember even some of what she said before she got you out on that balcony. I want to throw the book at her.

Lee broke his silence around midnight and had my deputies call me to come talk to him. He fingered Sylvia as the ringleader of the art thefts. He made a deal that will take the death penalty off the table for him in Melodie's murder trial."

Landry smiled and reached in her pocket. "Here. I sure hope it recorded ok through my thin sweatpants." Wyatt's mouth dropped open and he looked shocked. "You mean…?" Landry said, "Yep. She confessed to everything and even implicated her brother, Victor, and others in town." Wyatt threw his head back and cackled. "You are the best, Landry."

"Thanks. Now, can you tell me how you knew what was happening here? I was praying so hard that you would get to me but I just didn't see how that was possible since I had told you and everybody else that I was just going to bed early."

"You remember we were talking about Mr. Mayhew the other day? Well, we all owe him a huge apology for even thinking anything bad about him. Let me get him so he can tell you what happened tonight." Wyatt stood up and walked across the room and said something to Glenn Mayhew and they both came back over to where Landy was sitting.

"Miss Burke, I sure am glad that you are alright. I was so worried." He said.

"Mr. Mayhew, what happened tonight?" She replied.

"Well, I managed to get back in town around 10pm and as I came in from the garage, the installers of the security cameras from my company were just leaving. They stopped me and asked if they could give me the monitor for the cameras since it was late and they didn't want to disturb you. They said that everything looked like it was working properly. I told them yes, that I would give you the monitor in the morning and help you hook it up in your office so that you could monitor the lobby and halls if you needed to at night. Now, I hope you don't mind, but when I got in my apartment, I hooked the monitor up to my computer just to be sure that none of the cameras needed adjusting or anything. That's when I saw this lady come through the lobby doors. I knew that she didn't use a pass key since I saw her just open the door. She got on the elevator and I checked the other cameras to see who she was visiting. I was shocked when she got off on our floor and knocked on your door. When you let her in, I figured that she was a friend of yours. For some reason, I was still uneasy, though."

Landry spoke up, "That was you that I heard then. I mean, I thought I heard the elevator door open when I was talking to Sylvia on the phone. I decided it was my imagination and told her she could come by to see me. I think it spooked me a little to hear that when I knew that you and Ms. Scott weren't in the building."

"Yes, that was me. I wasn't expecting to be able to make it back into town tonight." he said.

"Tell her about what happened next, Glenn." Wyatt prompted him.

"Oh, yeah. Well, like I said I still felt uneasy about the

strange lady coming to your apartment late at night. I knew I wouldn't sleep unless I made sure you were ok. I came down the hall and was about to knock on your door when I heard a loud scream."

"That was me and Sylvia screaming when the thunder clapped so loud and the lightning was so bright in the living room." Landry said.

"Well, that's when I felt that something was wrong. I hit the stairs running and called 911. I told them to get the Sheriff's Department on the line. I explained everything to the desk deputy and he relayed it to the Sheriff, who was there taking a statement from a suspect. I stayed downstairs to open the front doors for them. They came in with sirens blaring and lights blazing. I was so relieved to see them. I could have knocked on the door myself, but since I didn't know just what was going on, I thought I better let law enforcement handle it." Mr. Mayhew explained.

Landry thanked him profusely and told him that she was so glad that he had decided to check the monitor when he got to his apartment.

Then, she looked at Wyatt. "How did you get into my apartment with the door locked?"

"Thankfully, you didn't have the deadbolt turned or the chain on it. I kicked it in. Amazing what adrenaline can do. Landry, when I walked out on that balcony and saw you about to go over the ledge, I froze. It scared me to death." Wyatt looked so serious when he said that.

"Awww…I love you too, my friend." Landry hugged him. "Thanks for rescuing me."

Adam was in the chair across from the sofa. "Hey. What about me? I carried you to the sofa." He said sarcastically.

Landry got up and walked over to him. About halfway there, she realized that every muscle she had was yelling at her. She could just imagine what her hair looked like after blowing in the wind and rain over the side of that railing. She didn't even care. She sat down in the chair beside Adam and said, "I love you too, my friend. I am so fortunate to have such wonderful people in my life." Adam smiled.

Right then, they both heard somebody outside the door of the apartment. "Let me in. That child is like my own. I gotta see with my own eyes that she is alright. Get outta my way."

They all looked at each other just as Ms. Millie blew into the room. She ran over and grabbed Landry and pulled her into a huge hug. "Oh, Jesus. Thank you so much for saving this child. She knows not what she does, Lord. She needs extra looking after."

Landry laughed and hugged her back. "Thank you Ms. Millie, I love you, too. I will admit that I was as scared as I have ever been for myself. I thought I was a goner there for a minute. How did you find out what was going on?"

Ms. Millie looked at her. "I have my ways. Now, child, you look horrible and you are shaking all over. Let me go get you a robe to put on. I will stop by the bathroom and get you a washcloth, too. You need to wipe your face off." Landry smiled at her and then it hit her. Just as Ms. Millie opened the bedroom door, Landry yelled, "No, Ms. Millie."

It was too late. Ms. Millie was backing out of the room and Zep was licking her ankles. Ms. Millie was saying, "Get away from me, beast. Just leave me be. I don't want no trouble." Of course, Zep had been shut up in the bedroom for a long time and just wanted to play. He kept licking.

Ms. Millie ran and sat beside Wyatt. "I want you to arrest that dog, Wyatt." Wyatt laughed. "What for, Ms. Millie?" Ms. Millie looked dead serious when she said, "Attacking me." Wyatt cleared his throat and said, "Uh…he only licked your ankles and he is now over there checking on Landry to be sure she is alright."

She looked over at Landry. Zep was jumping up and down in her lap, wagging his tail very fast and licking her all over the face. Ms. Millie could hear him whining and saw him snuggle his nose in Landry's neck.

Zep took that moment to jump from Landry's lap. Faster than a speeding car, he ran and jumped into Ms. Millie's lap. She screamed loud and grabbed Wyatt's arm. Then something strange happened. Zep just sat there and looked up at her. He didn't move or lick her or anything. She began to pet his head and then felt his fur. She looked over at Adam and said, "I don't know why you are so scared of this darling little puppy, Adam. He is so sweet. Look at him, just as sweet as can be. You should be embarrassed for being afraid of something this sweet." She continued to pet Zep and smile at him.

Adam looked very confused and said, "But, Ms.

Millie, Zep and I are friends and I am not afra…"

"Nevermind now. I am going to see if this little sweetie has food and water down." She got up and Zep jumped down and followed right behind her. Landry looked at the scene in shock.

Wyatt stood up and said that he was going to the Department to listen to the recorder that Landry had given him and start getting charges filed. He also had to call some officials in Europe to get Sylvia's brother in custody and then see what deal he might make with some of the ones they had in jail so that they could find all of the others across the country that were involved.

"I still think it is sad that Fred was killed because he was trying to stop Sylvia from stealing Aunt Tildie's painting. He was loyal to her even after she died." Landry dropped her head. "And, no matter what Melodie did, it wasn't enough for her to lose her life."

Wyatt left and so did the other deputies that were still there. Ms. Millie said she was going to walk out with Wyatt to her car just in case there were more bad guys out there that we didn't know about. Landry gave her a hug and told her she would see her on Monday at the bookstore.

It was almost 2am by the time everyone had left except for Landry and Adam. He looked at her and said, "Go get a hot shower. I will make us some hot chocolate and then you can take some medicine and go to bed. You, Miss Burke, are going to be very sore for the next few days."

She went and got a shower and stood underneath the hot water and thanked the Lord that she was still with the living. It hit her then just how close she had come to being pushed off of that balcony by Sylvia. She started crying and shaking and stayed in the shower until the water was turning cold. She got out, dried off and put on clean pj's and a pair of socks. She didn't even bother drying her hair. She pulled it up in a ponytail and would let it air dry.

She went to the kitchen and Adam handed her the cup of hot chocolate. "Mr. Mayhew helped me to put your door back on the hinges. It closes and will do for tonight. I'll get Lenny or Carl to fix it tomorrow. For tonight, I'm staying in the den. I have already pulled out the sofa bed and found some sheets and other bedding from the hall closet."

Landry started to say something and he stopped her by putting up his hand. "Don't. Your door is hanging on by a thread and you were knocked around pretty good tonight on that balcony. No way am I leaving you here by yourself. Now, drink that and take some medicine. Go to bed. I will see you when you wake up tomorrow."

It was still storming outside and Landry smiled to herself. She had planned on a quiet, peaceful evening of reading. She remembered what Aunt Tildie used to say, "Tell God your plans and watch Him laugh." She went to bed.

Chapter 24

Landry woke up to her phone ringing. She reached for it on the nightstand and immediately felt the effects of last night's nightmare. She was having spasms in her back and arms. Her legs felt so heavy she could hardly move them. "Hello?"

"Hello, Landry. It is your Mother. You do remember you have one, don't you?" Landry fell back on the pillows. Just what she needed today.

"Yes, Mother. I do remember. I was just waking up when you called." She groaned at the pain she felt from her body.

"What is wrong? Are you ill? You never sleep late. Why didn't you call to tell me you are sick? Should I hire a nurse to come be with you?" Not, 'Should I come home to be with you?' Landry noticed.

"No. I am just very sore. There was an…incident last night. Oh well, let me just fill you in." Landry sighed and told her Mother the entire horrid story.

Claire was silent the entire time Landry was telling the story. Then, when she did speak, she said, "You must leave that awful place now. You can come here, to Paris, with me. It sounds like you are in a war zone there. Murders, thefts, guns, knives, and YOU found the bodies. Yes, I will call and make arrangements with my travel agent. You will come over here. You can probably find a job at one of the historical libraries here. What a wonderful experience for you. What day do you want me to book your flight?"

"No. Absolutely not. This is my home now and I love it. It is not a war zone. It is a gorgeous mountain town and I own two businesses here. Besides, I have to watch out for Ms. Millie." Landry told her.

"Ms. Millie is still there? I thought she might have gone to live with her daughter, especially since Tildie passed away. They were as tight as ticks." Times like these are when Landry was glad that Claire was distracted so easily.

"Yes, she is still here. In fact, she is the manager of Jasmine Bloom, Aunt Tildies bookstore. Anyway, I have made new friends and I am not leaving…"

There was a knock on the bedroom door. "Are you decent?" Adam yelled from the other side of the door.

"Yep." she replied. He came in and didn't notice that she had her cellphone in her hand. He sat a cup of coffee on the nightstand and said, "I heard you talking to Zep and I thought you could use a cup of coffee. I thought I would take him for a walk since the rain stopped about two hours ago. Oh, and Carl came and repaired your door early this morning. It's good as new."

"Who is that?" Claire demanded. "Is that a man in your bedroom, Landry Margaret Burke? How could you? No wonder you don't want to leave that horrible town."

Landry looked at Adam, rolled her eyes and said, "This is my Mother on the phone. Thank you so much for taking Zep out. I will be up when you get back with him."

She waited for Adam to pick up Zep off of the bed and

said, "Mother, that is Adam Wilcox. He was Aunt Tildie's attorney and he is my friend. He offered to sleep in my den last night after all of the commotion since the Sheriff had to kick in my apartment door to get to me and they couldn't fix it until this morning. He is taking Zep out for a walk."

"Who is Zep? Does this Adam have a child? I cannot even keep up with you anymore, Landry." Claire sounded disgusted. Whether with herself or Landry was the question. Claire very well couldn't keep up with her daughter if she was in a different country every month.

"No. Zep is my dog. He was actually the puppy of the man who was killed in my building and I adopted him after his owner was gone. He is a cutie-pie." She smiled to herself just thinking about Zep.

"You have given me a throbbing headache. I must go do my yoga to relieve the stress. Please don't find anymore bodies, Landry, and don't put yourself in front of a gun again. Call me sometime. Au revoir." and she hung up.

Landry drank her coffee and then tried to get up to go to the bathroom. It was extremely hard to move. She made it there slowly. She brushed her teeth, washed her face and put her hair up as well as she could since she could barely raise her arms. She went into the kitchen and refilled her coffee and then went right back to lay in bed.

When Adam and Zep came back, he brought her a bagel and cream cheese from the diner. She wolfed it down since she was starving. "How did Zep do?" she asked Adam.

"He did good. We ran into another guy walking a

really big dog and Zep got right next to my leg and wouldn't move. I think he was a little intimidated." he laughed, looking at Zep who was sticking his head up in the air like he was saying, "No, I wasn't buddy. Nobody scares me."

"Be glad it wasn't a cat. Those do not intimidate him. Listen, Adam, I am hurting pretty bad. It is just my muscles, but I think I need to take some acetaminophen and just rest today and tomorrow. Would you mind dropping back by this afternoon and taking Zep out again?"

"Not at all. Uh, you have a pretty good bruise on your neck. Might want to put an ice pack on that. I am so sorry Sylvia hurt you like that, Landry." Adam looked angry. "I would have given anything to have been here in the den when she came here. In fact, I was planning on going over to Mom's and telling her what happened last night before she hears about it from somebody else. She will be so upset to hear what happened to you and it will be worse if it doesn't come from me. Then, I thought I would run by my house and do a few things there and grab some items I need. I will stop by the Takeout King and get us some food and come back here to eat with you. I can take Zep out for a walk then. I plan to stay here again tonight."

"You really don't need to do that, Adam. I am fine now and nobody is out to kill me since Sylvia and her gang are in jail. I will be alright here alone tonight."

"Sorry, but I won't be able to sleep if I know you are here in pain by yourself. I'm going to bring some things to make us breakfast tomorrow. I hope you at least feel a little better by then. Do you think you need to be checked out by a doctor? I can take you." He asked.

"No. I am just sore. I think I am going to lay here and read while you go run your errands. When you leave, please let Orvis know that I am alright but that I am not going out today. Ask him to call me on my cell if he needs anything so I won't have to walk to the living room to answer the intercom. Oh, and I am not sure if it is Maisy's or Jenna's Saturday to work but please drop by Jasmine Bloom and let them know that I won't be coming over there today and make sure they don't need anything."

"Got it." He walked into the bathroom and brought her the bottle of medicine. "Take this since you just ate. I will get everything done and be back later. Anything else you want me to pick up?"

Landry ducked her head and said, "If you find any ice cream while you are out, I wouldn't object to that." She laughed and he left.

She picked up her phone and called Annie. After she had told her the whole sordid story, Annie whistled and said, "My word. It seems like that town is a lot more interesting than Bent Branch. Landry, thank goodness you are alright. I will have to thank Mr. Mayhew for saving my best friend's life when I meet him. I am in shock about all of this. I thought you moved to a quiet little mountain town."

"I did. Don't sound so much like my Mom. She thinks I live in a war torn country. I love it here, Annie. One day, when you can visit, you will see why. It really is a beautiful place."

They talked for about an hour and finally said goodbye. Landry took her medicine and layed down to read. Her back felt like somebody had taken a wrench to it and twisted it every way it was not supposed to go.When she woke up, it was dark outside. Zep was laying at her feet snoring. She got up, stopped by the bathroom and went to the den. Adam was sitting on the sofa with his laptop open concentrating on whatever he was working on. He looked up and saw her. "Well, sleeping beauty, how are you feeling?"

"I feel better, actually. Why didn't you wake me when you got back?" She said gingerly in a chair.

"I didn't want to disturb you since I didn't know how long you had been sleeping. I took Zep out and he came back and ate his food and drank lots of water. He didn't want to leave your side, you know." Landry smiled and he continued, "I got us a plate from the Takeout King. They had a special tonight of meatloaf, mashed potatoes, fresh corn and a biscuit. I also got you some ice cream and put it in the freezer. When you get ready to eat, I will heat up the food."

"You are a great friend, Adam. And, I am ready now. I need to take some more medicine and I don't want to take it on an empty stomach. You should have gone ahead and eaten. You must be starving."

"Nah. You know my Mom fed me when I dropped by the B&B. She wouldn't let me leave without eating." He laughed. "But, that was hours ago and I am hungry. Let's go to the kitchen."

They ate their food and talked with some soothing music in the background. Adam said that he had gone to see Wyatt to find out what was going on with the investigation. Wyatt told him that they were all blaming each other until Sylvia found out that her entire conversation with Landry had been recorded and turned out clear as a bell. Wyatt was so happy with that and said that they all had confessed and that law enforcement all over the US was looking for the others involved.

"He is still baffled by something, though. Even though they all confessed to murders, thefts and other charges, none of them admitted they put the notes under your door. They all swear they don't know anything about that." Adam told her and Landry looked puzzled.

The next day, she was feeling almost back to normal. Adam picked up Judith for church and they came by and picked up Landry. It was a very nice day and after church, they all went back to the B&B where Judith had cooked a roast and some sides for them. They ate and sat on the porch in the rocking chairs and talked for a good long time. Adam took Landry back home and walked up to the apartment with her. He gathered his things that he had there and told her that he would see her tomorrow if she felt up to being out and about.

Monday morning, she got up, showered and dressed. She took Zep on a walk and brought him back. She went down to the lobby and Lisa and Garrett both started asking her questions at the same time. She sat down at Lisa's desk and told them all the details. Wyatt and Adam walked in at the same time. Wyatt said that several of the other players in the art theft scheme had been arrested including Sylvia's brother, Victor. They would be put away for a very long time. Wyatt scratched his head and said, "I still can't get any of them to confess to writing those notes that were put under your apartment door, Landry. It is just a puzzle to me."

Garrett cleared his throat but didn't look up. "Uh…I am afraid I am responsible for those notes."

Every person in the lobby stood there with a look of shock on their face as he continued, "I was worried about you, Miss Burke. I heard you talking to Lisa about trying to help solve the murders and I couldn't bear it if something were to happen to you. I thought those notes would make you stop looking into it and leave it to Sheriff Collins."

Wyatt finally spoke, "Garrett, I ought to arrest you for interfering with an investigation. Or, at the very least, sending threatening notes."

"Oh, please, Sheriff, don't do that. Doris would divorce me and I would have to go live in a cave. My reputation would be ruined." Garrett pleaded.

Landry spoke up, "Wyatt, if you read the notes, there was nothing threatening in them. They were just asking me to please stay out of it. He even said "please."

"Ah, I was just joking. Just don't do anything like that again, Garrett. Go to Landry in person and tell her what you need to tell her. By the way, we didn't find any foreign DNA on those notes. How did you manage that?" Wyatt asked Garrett.

Garrett reached into his jacket pocket and produced his white gloves that he wore regularly to check for dust on the furniture in the hallways on the floors. "I have several brand new packs of these at all times."

Wyatt couldn't help himself. He threw his head back and gave a roaring laugh. "I should have known, Garrett. I should have known." He turned to leave when a man with a huge bouquet of flowers walked in.

"Lisa Wilcox?" The man looked at Landry.

"Uh, no. That's Lisa there at the desk." Landry pointed to Lisa. He turned around and said, "Ok. These are for you, Lisa. Please sign here." She signed and took the flowers.

Landry, Adam and Wyatt all looked at each other. "Wow. They are gorgeous. Who are they from, Lisa?" Landry asked. Lisa looked up from smelling the flowers, smiled and said, "Wouldn't you all like to know?"

Wyatt left and headed to the Sheriff's Department. Adam and Landry headed over to the bookstore to see Ms. Millie. "Wonder who those were from?" Adam asked.

Landry replied, "I have no idea. Looks like we have another mystery to solve in Bobwhite Mountain."

THE END

RECIPES

FRIED OKRA

Ingredients:
Fresh okra
Self rising cornmeal
All purpose flour
Salt and Pepper
Vegetable oil for frying

-Wash your okra thoroughly. Cut the ends off the okra and slice into small round pieces (about ½ inch each). Put your cut up okra in a bowl and salt and pepper.

-Pour enough buttermilk (you can use regular milk if you don't have buttermilk) over the okra to moisten it. Not too much!

-Put about a cup (more or less depending on how much okra you have cut up) of self rising cornmeal to the bowl of cut up okra. Add a small amount of plain flour to the bowl. (About 3 tablespoons)

-Mix all of this up with a large spoon to bread your okra. Landry says that you don't want it to be sticky. It needs to be dry when you fry.

-Put the oil in a pot. (Landry uses a cast iron dutch oven.)

-You can check the oil to see if it is ready by putting one piece of the okra in the oil. If it bubbles and starts frying, it is ready. (Landry uses a long wooden spoon for this process. Just stick the handle of the wooden spoon in the oil. If it starts bubbling right away, the oil is ready.)

-Put in a little of the okra at a time to cook. (Landry says you don't want to cool the oil down in between batches.)

-Cook until golden brown and take out with a slotted spoon. (Landry uses a spider strainer.) Then, put on a paper towel to drain.

CRAB MEAT AU GRATIN

Ingredients:

2 tbsp butter

½ cup chopped onion

1 cup shredded cheese

1 cup milk

2 tsps creole seasoning

1 lb lump crabmeat

Hot sauce to taste

-Preheat your oven to 350 degrees

-In a medium saucepan (Landry uses cast iron), melt the butter

-Add the onion (cook until tender)

-Add the flour and cook while stirring until it is nice and light brown

-Slowly stir in the milk and cook all of this until it start to thicken up, then stir in half of the shredded cheese, the creole seasoning and hot sauce (how much depends on your taste)

-Reduce heat to low and cook just until the cheese is melted.

-Put in the crabmeat (Landry says she has used canned crab meat as well as imitation for this recipe)

-Grease a baking dish and pour the mixture in. Sprinkle the rest of the shredded cheese on top

-Cook for 20-30 minutes until you see it bubbling around the edges

-Landry says she serves this as a meal with salad and

garlic bread. She has also eaten it as a dip on crackers.

POSSUM PIE

Ingredients:
30 crushed round snack crackers (Landry put them in a freezer bag and crushes them with a rolling pin
3 egg whites beaten stiff with mixer
1 cup sugar (plus 2 tbsps)
1 tbsp vanilla flavoring
¾ cups chopped nuts
1 container whipped topping (thawed)
1 pack of sweetened coconut

-Preheat oven to 325 degrees
-Beat egg whites until stiff; add sugar, vanilla, crushed snack crackers and nuts.
-Grease a pie plate
-Pour mixture into grease pie plate
-Bake for 25 minutes
-Cool thoroughly (Landry says this is the most important part)
-Put whipped topping on top of pie
-Sprinkle coconut on top of whipped topping
-Let stand in refrigerator overnight
Landry says to be sure and bake two pies when you make this. She says that Adam could eat an entire pie by himself!

CHICKEN & DRESSING IN A CROCK POT

Ingredients:
4 boneless skinless chicken breasts
½ tsp seasoned salt
½ tsp black pepper
16 oz box of stuffing mix
½ cup sour cream
¼ cup mayonnaise
10.5 oz can of cream of chicken soup
⅓ cup water (Landry uses reduced sodium chicken broth)
10 oz package of frozen green beans

-Wash chicken breasts and season with seasoned salt and pepper; put in crock pot
-Dump the box of stuffing on top of chicken
-Mix together in a bowl: sour cream, mayo, soup and water (or broth) and pour on top of dressing
-Scatter the frozen green beans on top and season with salt and pepper
-Put the top on the crock pot and cook for 5 hours on high.
-Landry serves this with some cranberry sauce and rolls to complete the dinner

ACKNOWLEDGEMENTS

Special thanks to Author KC Hart for her advice and encouragement. She is a true angel on this earth.

Thank you to Julie Hatton, my wonderful cover designer. I love her work!

Many thanks to Author Sharon Brownlie (or as I like to call her, my Formatting Editor). Believe me when I say I could not have done this without her.

To my late Momma and Daddy: This is only possible because you always told me that I could do and be anything I wanted to. Thank you for always encouraging me and most of all for believing in me even when I didn't believe in myself. I miss you both so much.

To my brother, Ricky, thanks for always asking me "Day, you wanna plak (play like) we are…" You helped to fuel my imagination from an early age. Also, thanks for not killing me with all of your crazy antics when we were little so that I could still be here today to write this book. LOL!

Lastly, to my husband and daughter: Wow! What a ride this has been. You have both put up with my craziness and "Lucy Moments" for a long time. You have both also encouraged me to do this for years and have heard about the invisible friends of my imagination forever. Thank you for not brushing that off as me being off my rocker, lol. There is no way I would have ever done this without you both pushing me beyond my limits and supporting me to achieve my dream. Meg, you are the absolute BEST daughter in the world. I don't know what I would do without you by my side. It's pretty cool to give birth to your best friend! I love y'all and I am so thankful that God blessed me with both of you. Get ready for the next adventure…another book is bubbling in my brain.

ABOUT THE AUTHOR

Jamie Rutland Gillespie was born and raised in a tiny, country town in South Carolina. At the age of 18, she moved to a slightly larger town in the same state and still lives there. She spent much of her youth visiting the beaches of the lowcountry and taking trips to the mountains of North Carolina and Tennessee. The mountains were always her "happy place" and she still visits there whenever she has the chance.

Jamie has always loved to read. She got her library card at the small library in her hometown at the age of 6. She has a vivid imagination and has always made up stories in her head of places, people and situations that exist only in her head.

She currently lives in South Carolina with her husband, daughter and her 17 year old YorkiePom, who is her baby. She is still an avid reader and loves writing books, doing crossword puzzles, baking and spending time with her family.

Made in the USA
Monee, IL
13 June 2022